Sam wished ... ck to work abo ... on call tonight. Not on call, but always on duty, as the gun in his ankle holster reminded him.

His mother's Italian accent expressed a sense of excitement that Sam had no desire to feel right now. "Jessica Mathers, this is our son, Samuel. He's a detective with the Colorado Springs Police Department."

Jessica's mouth tightened when she glanced up at him. "Yes," she replied, "we've met once, under not-so-wonderful circumstances."

So she remembers that night, too.

Jessica moistened her lips. "I hope this meeting will be a little less stressful...for both of us."

Books by Carol Steward

Love Inspired

There Comes a Season #27
Her Kind of Hero #56
Second Time Around #92
Courting Katarina #134
This Time Forever #165
Finding Amy #263

CAROL STEWARD

wrote daily to a pen pal for ten years, yet writing as a career didn't occur to her for another two decades. "My first key chain said 'Bloom where you're planted.' I've tried to follow that advice ever since."

Carol, her husband and their three children have planted their roots in Greeley. Together, their family enjoys sports, camping and discovering Colorado's beauty. Carol has operated her own cake-decorating business and spent fifteen years providing full-time child care to more than one hundred children before moving on to the other end of the education field. She is now an admissions advisor at a state university.

As always, Carol loves to hear from her readers. You can contact her at P.O. Box 200286, Evans, CO 80620. She would also love for you to visit her Web page at www.carolsteward.com.

FINDING AMY

CAROL STEWARD

Published by Steeple Hill Books™

Special thanks and acknowledgment are given to
Carol Steward for her contribution to the FAITH ON THE LINE series.

Dedicated to families searching for loved ones.
May the Heavenly Father be your support.

Acknowledgments

My thanks to Jeffrey Sweetin, Special Agent with the
U.S. Drug Enforcement Administration, and Dave Galyard,
School Resource Officer with the Greeley Police Department,
for helping me clarify the intricacies of he
wonderful jobs you do!

STEEPLE HILL BOOKS

Steeple
Hill®

ISBN 0-373-87273-9

FINDING AMY

Copyright © 2004 by Steeple Hill Books, Fribourg Switzerland

www.SteepleHill.com

Printed in U.S.A.

He that conceals his transgressions
shall not prosper: but whoso confesses
and forsakes them shall have mercy.
—*Proverbs* 28:13

CAST OF CHARACTERS

Detective Samuel Vance—He's successfully taken down his friend's would-be killer. Can Sam rescue a missing child…and not lose his heart to the girl's mother in the process?

Jessica Mathers—The single mother has lived with terrible pain since the car accident that left her widowed. She wouldn't be able to survive losing her precious little Amy.

Amy Mathers—Jessi's daughter is only three years old. Where could she be?

Deanne Jones—What reason did the physically scarred baby-sitter have for disappearing with Amy?

Detective Rebecca Hilliard—Her job was to find missing persons. But would her feelings for her ex-boyfriend Sam get in the way?

Chapter One

Detective Samuel Vance had seen Jessica Mathers before, too many times. One too many, anyway. Like the night her drunk of a husband died. It was nothing short of a miracle that the accident hadn't killed Jessica and her daughter at the same time.

Jessica greeted each single man at the engagement party with a champagne flute in her hand, then sipped the bubbly faithfully. The waiter stopped and offered a replacement for her empty glass; Jessica giggled and leaned close, but didn't take another. Her light-brown hair glistened in the soft light of the chandelier. Though a healthy-size woman, she seemed thinner every time he saw her.

Sam recalled the way she'd looked the night of the accident—bruise on her left jaw, cuts all over her face. He'd been the first on scene. Her husband died immediately. Sam had taken her vitals, then glanced into the back seat and his heart had raced. He looked for the baby belonging to the diaper bag. "There's a baby somewhere! Where's the baby?" He jumped away from the car and turned circles, shining his flashlight into the field. No one had believed him, but he hadn't given up. He'd been the one to hear the little girl's whimper.

Sam turned away, wishing he hadn't been the officer on call that night. "A Vance never forgets," his father used to tell him. How he wished he could. Hers had been the most gruesome accident he'd seen. He shook the memory loose and searched for the bride- and groom-to-be.

Love songs crooned for Adam and Kate, the couple whose engagement sparked the laughter and happiness tonight. But as Sam bit into a dainty appetizer, he realized he needed to vent some frustration. After arresting Dr. Lionel Valenti for shooting Adam Montgomery in Venezuela and assaulting Kate Darling, Sam should be elated. Unfortunately, Valenti hadn't been as cooperative as they'd hoped he would be during the questioning. Sam needed something more than suspicion to tie Valenti to the Diablo crime syndicate. Tension in the division was at a peak. After almost a week, neither Sam nor any of the other top-notch interrogators had gotten the doctor to crack.

Sam heard Jessica laugh. The kind of party-girl giggle that spread like a virus. He watched the man beside her turn to putty.

"You're looking awfully cranky tonight," Sam's ex-sister-in-law teased. Emily followed his gaze and smiled softly. "Interesting view, isn't it?"

He shrugged, dismissing her baited question. "Interesting to who?"

She nudged him. "I have news for you, Samuel, you're not that discreet. Face it, you Vance men don't look if you don't like the woman."

He glanced back at Jessica, angry that Emily had

caught him. He could try to deny Emily's accusation, but he'd never succeed. "There's an exception to every rule."

Emily's laughter bounced off the colonial pane windows surrounding the Broadmoor Hotel ballroom and practically shattered the crystal chandelier. Sam felt as if a spotlight had just turned on them. His dad glanced over and headed toward him and Emily.

Sam didn't want to talk business right now. Especially not when his parents were together. He had questions for his father that couldn't be asked, let alone answered in public. "Now look what you've done," he said, razzing Emily. He scoped out their proximity to the exits. "It's too far to the door to escape."

"Don't be silly, why would you want to do that? Look, your mom and dad are bringing the woman with them," Emily murmured before she complimented his parents. "They look so young and in love."

Sam turned away from the oncoming trio, intending to take the shortest route out of the ballroom. Leave it to an engagement to put his mother in matchmaker mode. She and Mrs. Montgomery were both anxious for their families to grow. "I'm leaving, care to join me?"

Emily followed. "Sam, what has gotten into you?"

"Let's just say it's business related. And the last thing I want to talk about tonight is work."

"You and your father have to learn to communicate now that he's retired, Sam. He's home. Make the best of it."

"He's here all right. In my face. On the job and off." *Just like Jessica Mathers.*

Sam looked over his shoulder, relieved to find his mother introducing his dad and Jessica to one of her bridge club buddies. He took Emily by the elbow and zigzagged through the elegant surroundings where all of Colorado Springs's socialites, and a few of the working stiffs like himself, gathered in party attire. Sam removed his sport coat, hoping to cool off outside.

Emily simply waited for further explanation.

Sam grumbled about the impromptu celebration. "I'm not much for these shindigs."

Emily gave him a dirty look, even as he opened the door to the terrace for her.

"Samuel Vance. You should be happy for them." Emily scolded him as only a "sister" could.

Unsuccessful at ignoring her scowl, he conceded. "I am happy. Believe me. I'm happier than anyone in this city that Adam and Kate are still here to celebrate."

"I hear the wedding's at the end of the month. Sounds like they're anxious to return to the clinic in Santa Maria de Flores. Now can you make a little better attempt to enjoy yourself?"

He shook his head. "My mood has nothing to do with the party. I told you that. And I'd rather drop the subject."

As if she knew better than to try to intervene between the Vance men, Emily remained silent. Sam looked to the heavens and said a prayer. The August sun dangled above Pikes Peak, promising a colorful sunset. That alone assured Sam that God was in control, tonight and every night.

It suddenly dawned on Sam that Emily's silence might have more to do with her divorce from his brother than anything else. Stress built up inside law enforcement personnel, issues that couldn't be shared, even with loved ones. Sometimes especially because they were loved ones. "I'm sorry, Emily, I shouldn't have said anything."

"That part of the Vance life just never goes away, does it. Everything's top secret."

Something in her comment sounded like a freshly opened wound. "You heard from Peter?"

Emily leaned against the planter filled with bright red geraniums and tiny white flowers. Her voice softened. "No, I gave up on that long ago. You don't expect anything from an undercover agent. That way you're not disappointed."

"Even a do-better like you won't make it to heaven telling lies like that, Doc." He reached out and offered a brotherly hug. "You have every right to be disappointed. We just have to trust God is watching over Peter, wherever he is."

"Sounds like too serious a conversation for a party." Sam's mother stepped between them, as if suggesting something clandestine was going on. "Lovely party, isn't it?"

Sam and Emily both nodded obediently.

Lidia placed her hand on Jessica's arm and looked at Emily. "Jessica Mathers, this is Dr. Emily Armstrong, our son Peter's ex-wife. She's still one of the family."

Jessica's rose-colored lips twitched. "It's a pleasure to meet you, Dr. Armstrong."

"Drop the formalities, please." Emily greeted her mother-in-law with a hug while talking to Jessica. "It's nice to meet you." Emily glanced at Sam and silently chuckled. "It's nice to finally put a face to all the stories I hear about your work at the Women's Shelter."

"Thank you. I couldn't do much without our wonderful volunteers," Jessica said, carefully keeping her focus on Emily.

"I've been meaning to call, but it's been incredibly hectic at the hospital now that the renovations are complete. Don't hesitate to put my name on your list. I'm not always available, but I'll be happy to do whatever I can to help. We have to do something to stop this epidemic of broken homes.''

Sam observed the instant connection between the women, wishing he could be paged back to work about now. He knew better than to hope for the impossible. He wasn't on call tonight. Not on call, but always on duty, as the gun in his ankle holster reminded him.

Though Sam purposely avoided looking at his parents, as if he were a ten-year-old awaiting the doom of a major scolding, he felt his father's forbidding figure standing guard, keeping Sam in his place. Some things never changed.

''I'll look forward to working with you on the next fund-raiser,'' Jessica said in a silky voice.

Sam counted the seconds until the firing squad confronted him with the one woman he longed to forget. His mother's Italian accent expressed a sense of excitement that Sam had no desire to feel right now.

''Jessica, this is our son, Samuel. He's a detective with the Vice, Narcotics and Investigations Division of the Colorado Springs Police Department. Sammy…''

Ouch. Now he *knew* he was ten again, and in huge trouble. He didn't even hear the rest of the introduction. When would his mother realize a detective didn't go by ''Sammy''? Somewhere in the distance he heard Emily chuckle.

Jessica's mouth tightened when she glanced up to him. Her almond-shaped eyes were dark with mascara and her lips a tempting shade of soft pink. Her eyes narrowed, as if she, too, wanted to turn and run.

''Yes,'' she replied. ''We met once, under not-so-wonderful circumstances.''

So she remembers, too.

Jessica moistened her lips. "I hope this meeting will be a little less stressful…for both of us."

Don't bet on it. Sam felt his heart beat faster. Suddenly it seemed as if they were standing in the middle of a desert, and the lake was just a mirage. "How are you doing, Mrs. Mathers?" Against his better judgment, Sam offered his hand.

"Pardon me for not shaking hands—my back is bothering me tonight. I'm sure it sounds strange, but lifting my arm is torture. Hopefully a week from now, that will change."

"Oh?" Emily interjected. "Are you having surgery?"

Jessica's eyes opened wide with surprise. "As a matter of fact, yes." She briefly explained how doctors felt the cage from her previous surgery may need to be removed. "While they're in, they're going to replace a degenerating disk. Hopefully between the two, it will relieve the pinched nerves." Being a physician, for her the abbreviated version wasn't enough, and Jessica had begun to explain more thoroughly when a page forced Emily to say goodbye.

No sooner had Emily deserted Sam than his parents proclaimed that they needed to talk to Mayor and Mrs. Montgomery. His mother reached up to kiss his cheek. "Give her a chance, Sam," she whispered. "Enjoy the evening, Jessica. We'll be in touch soon."

"Thank you, Lidia. I'll see you Monday for sure."

Sam resisted the urge to follow his father back into the hotel. See what he was really up to. For a retired G-man, he was certainly keeping odd company these days.

"Is this a bad time to talk, Samuel?"

The forced words from the frail and frightened-looking woman in front of him drew his full attention. "No," he said, shaking his head. "This is fine. As long as you call me Sam. Otherwise, I'll think I'm in trouble. What can I help you with?"

They were immediately interrupted by an old classmate he hadn't seen since their ten-year reunion, followed by an apparent special delivery of Jessica's drink.

Her smile wavered, and he thought for a minute that she was going to cry. She took a deep breath and paused to compose herself.

"It might be easier if we walked. Do you mind?" She took a sip from the flute and the color seemed to drain from her face. She strolled slowly, apparently in a lot of pain.

"A walk is fine." One thing he'd learned as a detective—he did whatever it took to get to the truth. Though he didn't care anymore what Jessica's truth might be, he'd been raised better than to walk away right after an introduction. Sam tossed his jacket over his shoulder, glad he'd chosen the ankle holster instead of securing his weapon in the small of his back.

"I hope you don't mind that I asked your mother to introduce us." She turned in one motion to face him, as if her head didn't move independently any longer.

"You did?" The thought puzzled him only half as much as it flattered him. Even though it shouldn't. A party-girl like Jessica would do nothing but cause trouble. His mother should know better than to try to set him up with a lush.

Jessica blushed. "Yes, I did. I've meant to stop by the station ever since the accident, but time goes so fast. Now I'm trying to get ahead at work so I can have a little time off after my surgery. I've seen you at the

Stagecoach Café a few times, but I didn't place where I'd met you until I saw your picture in the paper this week.'' She paused for a breath.

''Is there a problem?'' He could list a dozen off the top of his head, any of which she should have dealt with years ago, before marrying a louse like Tim Mathers.

Her feet shuffled a little more quickly, almost as if trying to avoid him. Sam took an extra long step to catch up with her pace.

''I went to the grief counseling sessions you suggested after the accident,'' she said.

They were part of the routine follow-up with the victims, providing them information that might help. In the case of the death of a spouse, it wasn't uncommon to need help working through emotions. ''I hope they made it a little easier.''

''Yes, Dr. Nagashima is wonderful. She's helped in ways I never expected. Things I didn't have the courage to deal with at times, but I feel much better now.''

He had suspicions about what she meant, but left it to her to delve deeper if she wanted. He still wondered if this was the reason she'd asked his mother to introduce them. As she said, she could have taken care of this at the station, with as little as a phone call, even.

''That's what the program is for.''

Jessica nodded slightly, then flinched. ''Yes. I guess it is, isn't it.'' She fidgeted with her purse, gingerly tilting her head from side to side and stretching her shoulders. ''Still, sometimes people are reluctant to take advantage of free services. I appreciated your suggestions.''

''No problem.''

"I see why your mother is so proud of you—you're a patient listener."

He wondered why Jessica and his mother had talked about him. "Goes well with detective work, I guess."

Jessica stopped, and Sam casually leaned a hip against the railing, watching her kick off her sandal and remove a pebble. Then she took off the other shoe and slowly bent down and picked them up. He cast an approving glance, noticing her nice tan and striking burgundy-painted toenails.

"I'm sure it's part of why you're so good at your job," she continued, totally oblivious to his observation. "I was more than a little surprised to find out that the cop who saved my daughter and me is in the church choir."

"It's only the keyboard, for the Praise Team, but close enough for government work."

She laughed. "I stand corrected. I tried to picture you trading in your uniform for a choir robe."

"Naw, I'm a little too much rock-and-roll for the traditional choir."

Her laugh was more relaxed. "You do look a little wild and dangerous, now that you mention it. Kind of a cross between a dark-haired Val Kilmer and Elvis."

Sam thought a moment, then shrugged, his shoulders feeling a bit broader. "Guess I can't argue with being compared to a music legend and a movie star, now can I." *Especially by a woman pretty enough to be in movies herself.*

Jessica took a step, then stumbled, as if she'd been stabbed by another pebble. Sam offered a hand to steady her. "Maybe the grass would be easier on your feet." He pushed away from the wrought-iron rail and guided her to the golf course adjoining the hotel property.

"Sure, that would be great." She stepped onto the lush lawn and smiled. "It's nice and cool, too. You ought to try it."

"I'm doing okay, thanks." The sooner they got back to the party the better. "This might be a good time to get to what you needed to talk to me about."

"I needed to…" Her voice faltered. The tension reappeared on her face, making her look five years older. "First of all, thank you for all you did the night of my accident."

"I was just doing my job." He really didn't want to discuss that night. Especially with her.

She turned slowly toward him. "No, something tells me you did just the opposite."

"What?" He'd done his job completely. What in the world did she think he'd done?

"I'm sure you assumed I was lying to you when I answered your questions. You were so adamant that Tim had been drinking. I honestly didn't know Tim had lost his license—" she took a couple of deep breaths "—or spent time in jail, until the insurance agent contacted me. I'm surprised that you didn't have to press some sort of charges. Against me, I mean."

He didn't have the courage to tell her he had considered it. He shrugged impatiently.

Jessica's quizzical look needed no explanation. "You had to have some reason."

"You…" He closed his eyes, trying to put the scene behind him. "I guess I figured you'd paid a high enough price, losing your husband. There was no need to make matters worse. What was done was done."

"All this time I've been expecting someone to show up at my door to press charges. Is that still a possibility?"

"No, the case is closed." What retort he expected, he wasn't sure. He'd been totally caught off guard by her matter-of-fact questions as well as his feeble answer. He paused, watching her stroll slowly ahead of him, her pain evident in the way she walked. He wondered now if he had done and said the right thing. "You can stop worrying. I presume the back problems are from the accident?"

She nodded. "It started then, and I'm sure lifting Amy so much doesn't help."

"Another surgery seems pretty drastic. Why do they have to go back in to take the…cage…out? Didn't it do what it was supposed to do?" He suddenly realized she might not like the intrusion into her privacy and raised his hand to stop her. "Forgive me. You don't have to…"

Jessica waved a hand, as if to brush his words away. "It's not a big deal. The cage stabilized my spine, but after it healed, the metal just seems to irritate it. They suspect the next disk is now causing the additional pain. After months of physical therapy, chiropractors, massage therapy and steroid injections, I'm just ready to get it over with so I can enjoy life again."

He stopped and looked at her, noting the shadows under her gray eyes. "Then, as of tonight, you can take one worry off your shoulders. No one is going to come after you. Your husband was at fault, and unfortunately, he paid a high price."

Her features softened with relief. "I wish it were that easy, but at least I can go into surgery without fear that my daughter could be taken away from me. It's really going to be okay?"

Sam felt about as tall as an anthill. He'd been set on discrediting this woman's husband, and all this time she'd been worried about being there for her daughter. "Yeah, it's going to be okay." This was the part of his job he hated—seeing the pain that one person's selfishness caused another. Justice came with a price, and it rarely stopped at the perpetrator of the crime. And now Jessica's child would grow up without her father.

No one ever guaranteed life was fair.

Chapter Two

A cool breeze whistled through the pine trees, offering much-needed relief from the heat. "Do you mind if I loosen my tie?"

Jessica laughed, hoping he didn't notice her interest in him. She held up her sandals. "You're asking me?" Sam probably didn't want to know that she wouldn't mind if he wore khaki shorts and a T-shirt. "I'm not much for formal attire, but these days, you do what it takes to keep a job that you love." Which reminded her of the real reason she'd been introduced to Sam. She watched him fumble with the knot of his tie and unbutton the collar, finding it quite odd that something so casual could make a confident man like Sam look uncomfortable.

"I hear you there." He sighed and his mouth curved into a devastating smile. "This breeze is a Godsend after the heat we've had this week. Eleven straight days of over a hundred degrees. That's one record I'd rather we never break again."

Jessica closed her eyes and breathed deep. "I could

do without the heat, but I miss the long days when summer ends. It's so nice to have time at the end of the day to go for a picnic or play at the park.''

"How is your daughter doing?''

Jessica felt a sudden warmth just thinking of Amy. ''She's doing well. She still won't talk much, but her pediatrician reminds me that she's been through a lot for a three-year-old.''

His quick smile crinkled the skin around his deep-brown eyes. ''You both have. I'm sure she'll come out of it soon.''

She felt like a blanket of comfort had been wrapped around her.

"I remember her golden pigtails,'' he added.

"How could you remember that?'' Jessica laughed. ''She barely had enough hair to get into tiny barrettes then, but she loved having her hair fixed. I just happen to have pictures, if you'd like to see them.''

"I'd love to.'' Sam stopped walking and motioned toward the park bench.

Sitting down, Jessica dropped her sandals to the grass and slipped them on. She pulled several snapshots from her bag, describing the pictures and who was with Amy in each. ''I'm a little possessive after that night. And much more appreciative.''

"As you should be.'' He took the offered pictures and admired them. ''Still has that golden hair and blue eyes. She's as beautiful as her mother.'' Sam stopped speaking suddenly, as if he hated complimenting her.

Jessica felt her skin flush, whether because of the compliment or his practically snatching it back, she wasn't sure.

"She's a precious little girl. It's amazing how a few seconds can change your life so drastically. I don't know how I'd have lived with the guilt if something had happened to her, too.''

Despite her ignoring his compliment, Sam's shoulders tensed and he edged away. She tried to ignore the pain his simple action caused her. They really didn't know each other, and she knew better than to take his comment too seriously. He was being so incredibly polite, letting her go on and on about Amy; the least she could do was not make an issue of his embarrassment.

Sam looked across the lake, his furrowed brow and five o'clock shadow intensifying that rock-star appeal.

''Something wrong?''

Sam acted as if she'd caught him spying on someone. He shrugged. ''I'm not sure. That looks like my dad.''

Odd, she thought. ''He is here, remember? I'm sure he and Lidia haven't left yet.''

''Oh, yeah. It's still early, isn't it.'' Sam eased back on the seat, though he continued to stare across the lake. ''It's strange having him in town all the time. He traveled a lot when we were kids.''

''I'm sure that is an adjustment. How is it having him home all the time?''

Sam thought a while. ''It's different. Nice, but a little strange. I've been so used to keeping an eye out for my mom and sister that I feel like I've been demoted or something.'' His brooding expression emphasized the tender side of Sam that she remembered, and she knew what Lidia admired about her youngest son. Lidia claimed he was the teddy bear of the family. He looked and acted tough, but was all mush inside.

Jessica found it difficult to build an image of a tough detective singing and playing an electronic keyboard. To say he puzzled her was an understatement. Right now, she'd give anything to see the teddy bear.

Jessica glanced at her wrist and realized she hadn't worn a watch. She hadn't thought the cartoon-character watch she usually wore would fit in at an exclusive hotel. "Do you know what time it is?"

Extending his arm, Sam exposed a fancy gold watch and took a quick glance. "About eight-fifteen."

She took another sip of her ginger ale. She hadn't seen Sam drink a drop. "Aren't you thirsty?"

"Yeah, but drinking alcohol is prohibited when I'm wearing a weapon."

Jessica waggled her eyebrows while examining his belt, puzzled that she saw no evidence of a gun. "A secret weapon, I presume?" She couldn't help but look again, embarrassed that she was staring at him.

He crossed one ankle over the opposite knee and smiled, pointing to a small leather holster and a gun. "Just like in the movies. Except in real life, officers don't drink alcohol while on duty."

She felt her cheeks turn pink and laughed at her ignorance. "Of course. Does your ballpoint pen blow up, or is it your hidden camera?"

He raised an eyebrow. "You watch too many movies."

"Only if there's an attractive hero in it." She offered her glass. "Would you like to finish my ginger ale? I'm really not thirsty, but the waiter has been so kind, bringing me refills, that I don't have the heart to decline another glass."

He looked shocked. "Ginger ale? Wish I'd thought to ask for a soda. It seemed like too much bother to ask for something special." He accepted the glass and guzzled it.

"So you'd rather go without." The pink hotel looked even brighter as the sun peeked above the mountain.

Jessica studied the sky. "What a gorgeous sunset tonight."

Sam leaned forward again, obviously too intent on the men outside the hotel to make small talk. He stood and motioned toward the ballroom. "I suppose we should head back."

"Oh, sure. It is about time I got home." Jessica put the snapshots back into her bag and started to stand. Sam put his coat on and offered his hand. She'd never met a man her age with such good looks and impeccable manners as well.

Jessica wondered how to broach the subject of the fund-raiser. Time was getting short and they were almost to the terrace. "Sam, there was something else I needed to talk to you about," she said, the words barely escaping her mouth. She needed to complete her list of participants before the surgery. If she didn't, publicity wouldn't get out until after her sick leave was over. She couldn't miss this deadline. This project was new to the Colorado Springs community, according to her committee members' recollection, anyway. She knew it could be successful. It had to go smoothly—for her career's sake, and for the well-being of the shelter.

Sam placed his hand around her waist just as she heard deep, angry voices. He pulled her into the trees.

"Sam, what's wrong—"

He placed a finger over her lips, then turned her back toward the terrace and leaned close. "Probably nothing, but I'd rather these two not notice us."

"Who?" Voices behind her got louder and Jessica turned.

Sam took her by the shoulders and pulled her close. "Don't look," he demanded softly.

"Excuse me?" She pushed against him.

His grip on her arms loosened, but he didn't let her move away. "Pretend to kiss me—maybe they'll think we're just guests at the hotel out for a romantic walk."

"Pretend..." He pulled her into his warm embrace and his face brushed near enough for her to feel that he needed to shave. "This is going to cost you."

"Whatever you want." His lips were a whisper away. So close she could feel the warmth of his breath. Her heart beat faster.

"You mean it?"

"Yeah, sure." He rested his strong hand on her waist and turned their bodies slightly, looking over her shoulder. "There, that's better."

His words faded suddenly as his lips met hers. For a man who didn't give a hoot about her, his kiss certainly packed a punch. Didn't matter, she told herself. She was about to return the favor the next time he let her come up for air. Before she knew it, the only noise she heard was the musical rhythm of her own heart.

She didn't notice the pain in her back. She didn't notice that the sun had completely dropped behind the mountains, or that the terrace lights had come on. For a minute she wondered if Sam had forgotten that this was a ruse. Then suddenly he pushed her away and looked around, seemingly convinced that they were alone.

"Think they fell for it?" She didn't know where she'd come up with the presence of mind to ask such a bland question when her heart was dancing.

He laughed. "Yeah, they're gone now. Sorry about that."

She smiled back. "Not a problem. You know what they say about paybacks..."

"What about it? Take you for coffee?"

"You're not even close," she said. "Very, very cold, in fact." Jessica shook her head and crossed her arms in front of her. "That's going to cost you. Big."

"What are you talking about?"

"As you may or may not know, I'm the Development Director at the Galilee Women's Shelter. In other words, I'm in charge of making enough money for the shelter to stay open. Since your mom is a volunteer, I'm sure she's told you about the fund-raiser next month."

He looked puzzled. "Other than talking my sister into helping with it, she hasn't given any details."

Jessica suspected as much. She also knew that Lidia was sure Sam would turn her down, which was why Jessica was here, getting kissed, which she hoped she didn't have to do with every participant. She could guarantee it wouldn't be nearly as much fun as kissing Sam.

He looked at her warily. "Why?"

"I need eligible bachelors, which you must be or you'd probably be very worried about someone seeing that kiss."

He looked either sick or angry, she wasn't quite sure which.

She raised her eyebrows playfully. "Trust me, it's for a worthy cause."

He shook his head immediately. "No."

Jessica glared at him and wiped her lips. "No? Did Sammy say no?"

There was no question now, he was angry.

"That kiss was as much for your protection as mine."

She laughed. "Right. And that is the worst pickup line I've ever heard."

"Trust me, Jessica…" His voice faded.

"I believe you said 'whatever you want' when I warned you it would cost you."

Sam pulled her out of the trees and walked toward the terrace. She felt completely safe in his hands, but couldn't deny how much she enjoyed having the advantage. She didn't imagine he was accustomed to being at a disadvantage in any situation.

"Just tell me what I owe you."

"Congratulations, Samuel Vance, you've been unanimously nominated to be one of Colorado Springs's most eligible bachelors in our bachelor auction. One lucky woman will be your guest on the dream date of your choosing."

The look on his face was priceless. His olive-hued complexion suddenly looked like he'd spent a month in the sun. His eyebrows drew together to form one black line above his deep-set brown eyes and the smile was long gone.

"You're expected to be one of the top moneymakers, if that helps any. And if that kiss was any indication, I'd say they're right."

Chapter Three

Sam couldn't imagine what had gotten into him. He wasn't the impulsive type. And party-girls like Jessica Mathers certainly weren't his typical weakness either. And even the hour or two he'd spent talking with Jessica blew that partying, lush image all to pieces. She hadn't even been drinking, as he'd presumed. Her glass had been filled with nothing stronger than ginger ale. Some detective he was—couldn't even tell champagne from soda. So what had she been drinking all those weeks at the café if she wasn't drinking wine? It certainly hadn't looked like ginger ale.

He'd be sure to ask his mother the next time they had lunch at the café. That is, unless his father decided to join them. The one part of his life that Sam would just as soon keep Dad out of was his love life—or lack of one. Max could not understand why Sam was still single at thirty-two. Sam couldn't help it that his parents had been lucky enough to find the right person the first go-round. Sam had discovered quickly what a rare woman his mother truly was—strong, patient, trusting and very capable of handling a houseful of kids all on her own. With his dad out of the country much of his childhood, Sam had grown especially close to his mother, which fostered uncommonly high expectations when it came time to choose a wife. Yes, his father was a lucky man. Sam could only hope to find such a treasure for himself. When he found the right woman—*if* he found her—he'd take all the time needed to make sure they were right for one another. According to his sister, Lucia, Sam would never find a woman to measure up to the outlandish expectations he'd set. Only God knew for sure.

It was too late to be outside shooting baskets. Where was his brother when he needed a sparring partner?

"How'd I get myself into this mess?" he mumbled as the impact of the evening set in. Of all the women, it had to be Jessica Mathers. Hoping not to bother the neighbors, he closed the windows and started the central air-conditioning, then turned on the keyboard. He played familiar rock-and-roll tunes that helped him release the pent-up frustration so he could clear his mind and focus on the praise music for tomorrow's service.

An hour later, he gave in to the fatigue and got ready to turn in. Sam tuned the radio to his favorite station, determined to get Jessica out of his head. Every time she drifted into his mind, he forced his thoughts elsewhere.

The replacement wasn't much easier to deal with tonight. Visions and voices ran a play-by-play of his father talking to Alistair Barclay, a man too smooth to be on the up-and-up. Barclay had blown into town a few years ago and started throwing his weight around, along with his money.

As a part of the Vice Division, Sam was well aware

of the increased drug activity in the city. With drugs
came countless other problems. And instinct told Sam
that Barclay was one man to keep an eye on. He drove
fast cars and had a harem of equally speedy escorts to
keep him company. Women with model figures and
faces to match were only interested in a sleaze like Barclay for one reason, and the red comb-over wasn't it.
Sam found it amazing what money could buy. A
woman's love and loyalty was the one thing Sam refused to pay for.

Jessica invaded his thoughts again, and he forced
himself to think about something easier to deal with,
like Alistair Barclay.

The hotels Barclay built had brought jobs to the community, making him an instant hero to many. Sam
didn't blame those so easily influenced during a struggling economy. On the surface, even he would agree—
Barclay almost looked good. He only wished he could
find substantial evidence to link Barclay's arrival to the
increase of crime in the community.

Sam just happened to be more suspicious than the
average citizen, which probably had more to do with
why he was home alone every night. Women seemed
to thrive on love, and love involved trust. Sam found it
next to impossible to put his trust in anyone else. He'd
seen what love had done to his brothers, what it did to
the women left behind.

Emily came to mind. She'd loved Peter, but even
then, love and trust weren't enough to overcome the
perils of a career filled with secrets. Travis's wife never
did adjust to the fact that her husband was a cop, and
Travis still lived with weight of guilt on his shoulders.

Sam shook his head and turned out the lights. Nothing killed a perfect romance like secrets. How could he

ever expect to find happiness with the odds stacked against him? His life, like his brothers' and father's, dealt mostly with lies and deception—rooting them out and upholding justice.

A certain brunette faded in and out of his mind as he drifted to sleep. Why couldn't he just forget her? She wasn't his type.

Every dream he'd had during the night came alive when he saw Jessica step through the precinct door with a springy bounce. Until she reminded him of the one thing he wanted desperately to forget...the bachelor auction.

"Afternoon, Sam. Ready to put together a dream date?" She'd obviously slept her aches away, or was on some pretty powerful medication. Her enthusiasm spread throughout the office as every detective in the building turned to see Sam's reaction.

"I don't remember setting an appointment."

She lifted her hands regretfully and smiled. "I really need to finalize your selections for the newspaper ad."

Sam leaned forward, instinctively defensive. "You didn't say anything about publicity."

Interest in their conversation grew by the syllable. "You wouldn't have heard me if I had. If I recall correctly—"

Sam jumped from his seat, led her into the captain's office and closed the door.

"Do you realize that I have a reputation in this city as a—" His words lost their punch when he discovered the amusement in her gaze. "A cynical cop, a—a respected officer. What will my fellow officers think?"

She laughed at him. He couldn't believe her nerve. Jessica leaned her head back, gazing into his eyes.

"There isn't a man out there who wouldn't trade places with you in an instant." She motioned to the outer offices and placed a hand on her hip. "And I have news for you, Sam. You aren't nearly as tough as you try to make people think you are. But that's okay, your secret's safe with me." She raised an eyebrow and smiled. "The tough silent type isn't nearly as attractive as Hollywood wants us to believe. Marriages in this country wouldn't be nearly as endangered if couples realized that honesty is far more desirable than physical appearance." Jessica lifted her briefcase to the chair and shook her head. "If I can convince half the women in the shelter of that, my own pain won't have been wasted. Now, so I don't waste any more of your valuable time, why don't we get to work?"

He couldn't believe she'd condensed his own opinions and verbalized them. It unnerved him. He'd never cared half as much about looks as he did personality. Had his mother told Jessica to say that? She must have. How else could Jessica have known?

There was no doubt in his mind who was on the other side of the door when that fist hammered on the glass. Sam backed his way to the entry, hoping the captain would appreciate the humor in the situation. His hand paused on the doorknob.

"Why don't we go to the Stagecoach for a cup of coffee and go through this?"

She stepped close. "You wouldn't be trying to get out of this, would you?"

"Vance! Out here, on the double." A loud voice resonated through the door.

The humor just left the office. "Honestly, I was, but since it's for such a good cause, I'll go through with it.'' Sam turned the doorknob. ''I'll call you to set up a time to meet.''

One eyebrow lifted and Jessica's gray eyes sparkled. ''I'll be waiting, but remember, I have to get this done before my surgery.''

Captain Sullivan's eyes widened in surprise when Jessica eased her way past him. ''Excuse me, Captain Sullivan.''

Sullivan eyed Sam, then Jessica. ''I didn't mean to interrupt, Ms. Mathers. Sam, I really am sorry to break this up, but we have a major problem in the jail.''

A major problem could only refer to one inmate— Dr. Lionel Valenti. ''I was on my way there. He's got to crack one of these days.''

Sullivan's grimace didn't leave much doubt what the problem was. ''Your suspect just became the victim. He's dead.''

''Suicide?''

''No, doesn't look like it.'' Sully nodded a greeting to Jessica and looked at Sam. ''When you're finished here, we need to get started on the investigation. Mayor Montgomery called the press. He's making a statement on the evening news. We need to be ready with an announcement before rumors get started. Jessica, good to see you again.''

She smiled. ''You, too, Captain. Sam, give me a call and we'll discuss what you'd like to do.''

''Let's make it over dinner at seven, and be sure to bring Amy. I could use a little laughter.''

Her astonishment was obvious as the words caught in her throat. ''Tonight? Where?''

''I'm not sure yet, I'll pick you up.''

''Do you…''

He laughed. "I'm sure I can find your address somehow. I have connections."

Sam watched her leave, dreading the job ahead of him. He would definitely need some cheering up tonight, even if it involved Jessica Mathers.

He and the captain spent the remainder of the afternoon on the Valenti homicide, interrogating other prisoners, jailers and guards. No one had seen anything suspicious. They examined the visitors' log and moved on to question the kitchen staff. It could be days before they'd know if anything showed up in the blood tests. The crime scene investigators finished taking pictures and logging the contents of Valenti's cell. Sam stayed behind, looking under the mattress and in every nook and cranny for anything that might have been hidden.

Once back at the precinct, Sam dug deep into each witness's profile, hoping to find some connection to the Diablo Syndicate, Venezuela, or local drug dealers. He couldn't believe they had a connection and he'd slipped right through their fingers. Sam contacted Valenti's next of kin, depressed to think that Valenti's parents had to hear the news from a total stranger, under such incriminating circumstances.

This job never got any easier.

He spent two hours on the phone with the director of Doctors Without Borders, trying to evaluate whether they had noticed any problems with Lionel Valenti before the burglary that injured Adam Montgomery. He kept digging, hoping someone could identify locals in the area that Valenti had been seen with when off duty.

Either Dr. Valenti led a very isolated life, or he was very adept at keeping secrets. No one seemed to have known anything about Valenti's personal life, who his friends had been, or where he'd lived.

Before Sam realized it, it was time to go to City Hall. The crew had set up the cameras and lights in the conference room. Colleen Montgomery, reporter for the *Colorado Springs Sentinel,* stood by as her father prepared for his speech. Mayor Montgomery stepped behind the podium and began by giving a picture-book description of Colorado Springs as the idyllic city.

"For the past year, however, we've experienced a drastic increase in violent crimes and drug-related violence." Montgomery encouraged the community to join together to help city officials work to bring justice to criminals. Twenty minutes later a local television reporter interviewed Sam for the evening news.

Jessica closed down her computer at the Galilee Women's Shelter, ready to call it a day. She locked the door behind her and shouldered the strap of her backpack, then walked past Susan Carter's door. "See you tomorrow, Susan," she said to the director.

"Come here a minute. You might be interested in this story on the news. The mayor is going to speak after the commercial."

"Mayor Montgomery? I wonder what is up?"

"I'm not sure, but I received an e-mail from his secretary requesting my attendance at a task-force planning meeting on Wednesday."

"Do you need coverage? I'll be here Wednesday, but not Thursday or Friday, remember?"

Susan nodded, sending her corkscrew curls into motion. "I have your sick leave on my schedule. Are you getting nervous about the surgery?"

"No, I'm so ready. I can hardly make it through the evening with Amy some nights. That's just not fair to her—"

Their conversation was interrupted by the return of the program. Mayor Montgomery's picture came on, and then they moved to clips from his speech. "Violence is like a virus—it mutates and spreads, and it will take over our city if we don't do something now. We are going to stamp out crime in Colorado Springs. Our law enforcement will work to eradicate domestic abuse, drugs…"

"That must be what the meeting is about," Susan said.

"They have a huge job ahead of them. I admire the mayor's determination. Someone has to do something."

As Jessica headed for the door, Sam appeared on the television screen. Jessica stopped to watch. She admired him, anxious to see him at dinner tonight. Even if it would be official business.

"That is one handsome man," Susan said with a teasing grin.

Jessica smiled. "I wouldn't dream of arguing with you. I'm sure he'll bring a pretty penny for the shelter's budget. Which brings me to say farewell. I need to get Amy home. We girls have a business dinner to get ready for."

Susan raised her eyebrows. "That sounds interesting. Keep me up-to-date on how it goes. And if you need any help finishing up the publicity, I'll be glad to get it to Colleen."

Just before seven o'clock, Sam called Jessica to confirm her address and see if they were still on.

"Surely you don't think you're going to be let off the hook? Took me long enough to get the courage to ask you to do this, Samuel Vance. Now that I have you, I'm not about to let you go."

"You sound awfully confident, Ms. Mathers."

"Do you want to be the one to tell your mother you backed out?"

He laughed. "Not a chance. But honestly, I can't believe that spending the evening planning a date for a bachelor auction is the highlight of my day. I'll be right over."

Chapter Four

Despite the tension of the murder investigation, a smile teased Sam's lips when he saw Jessica and Amy waiting in front of the two-story Victorian. He stopped the truck and walked around it to meet them.

"Evening, Jessica." He knelt down and smiled at the little girl. "Hi, Amy, I'm Sam, a friend of your mom's."

Amy giggled then ducked behind Jessica's leg.

"She doesn't talk much," Jessica explained. Amy held out her teddy bear for Sam to see.

Sam recognized it as the one he'd given her in the hospital. "That's a really cute bear. Looks like you love it a lot."

Jessica tousled Amy's windblown hair. "She takes it everywhere. Someone gave it to her after the accident."

He extended his hands, but Amy held on tight to her mother's leg. "Well, if you're ready to go... Amy, would you let me help you and your bear into the truck?"

Jessica glanced into the truck as she spoke. "I was

going to suggest we take my car since you don't…oh, you *do* have a child seat." She looked again in the truck and back at him. "I hadn't even considered you might have children."

He somewhat enjoyed watching "Miss Personality" fumbling for words, though it seemed peculiar. She hadn't seemed at a loss when he'd seen her lunching recently with those other men at the Stagecoach Café. "I brought one from the station. We keep them on hand, in case we need to transport children."

She bit her lower lip, wrinkled her nose for a second and looked at him, her expression full of appreciation. "What made you think of bringing one?"

"It's my job to plan ahead. I figured it would be easier this way. Are you ready? I'm starving." Sam motioned to the truck and opened the passenger door.

As Jessica stepped back, Amy moved with her. "Don't tell me you got so caught up in the investigation that you didn't have lunch?" While Jessica pried Amy's arms from around her legs, Sam noted her disapproving glance. "Amy, we're going to eat now. Can you let Sam help you into his big truck? Mommy's back hurts."

Amy nodded. "Mommy owie."

He offered Amy a hand, and she lifted both arms up to him. "Can you say 'Sam,' Amy?"

Amy smiled and gave Sam a hug.

"Wow." Jessica's slate-colored eyes opened wide. "You should be flattered." She apparently hadn't expected Amy to respond so well to him. "What did you do, give her *C-A-N-D-Y* when I wasn't looking?" She gave him a wink as she moved to the truck and set her briefcase on the floor beneath the car seat.

As she stepped back, Sam reached up and grabbed the door, blocking her in the small triangular opening with him and Amy. "Kids are a good judge of character. I don't need to bribe her." Jessica's eyes brightened with her usual perkiness. "Must just be that natural charm, huh?"

"Must be. Only works on certain females, though."

She blushed, then ducked under his arm, skimming her hand along his ribs. "That's what you think, Samuel Vance."

"What's that supposed to mean?" While he waited for another of Jessica's smart-aleck remarks, he gently set Amy in the seat and helped position the straps over her shoulders. Amy grabbed the buckle, as if she thought she could do it herself. Sam waited until she took his hand and guided it to the buckle. "Need help?"

Amy nodded. Sam snapped the locks in place, then tested the seat to make sure it was secure. "I asked around the precinct for suggestions on where the car seat works best. There isn't enough room in the back seat. Sometimes kids kick the gearshift when they're in the middle, so the passenger seat won the vote. I turned off the air bags, so that's safe."

"Sounds like you have everything under control."

"Not quite everything. You didn't answer my question."

Her pink cheeks were answer enough for him.

"Nor do I plan to." Jessica wished she had an on-off switch to her heart. Sam's charm could be considered a lethal weapon. And this wasn't even a date, it was a business dinner.

"Plan to what? Answer me honestly, or fall for my charms?" He stepped around her, glancing up the street, then back at her with a boyish smile. Sam opened the driver's door and the half door to the back seat, lifted the bench seat, placed his service pistol inside a lockbox and closed it. That told her a lot about him. "Knowing I had plans with you and Amy got me through the day."

She hated avoiding his questions, but her feelings for Sam were difficult to explain. She remembered his compassion from the accident as well as his determination to get to the truth, no matter the cost. She'd seen him a lot recently at the café where she'd met with the other bachelors. She presumed he was there to meet a wife or girlfriend. Then, after his mother mentioned introducing them and an article in the newspaper about his capturing Adam Montgomery's assailant, Jessica had put the pieces together. Sam had been going to have lunch with his mother. "I saw you on the news tonight. How did the investigation go?"

Sam shook his head. "I've had better days. If I hadn't had a date planned, I'd probably have grabbed a burger and worked straight through."

"You have to go back to work after dinner?" She turned, suddenly aware of the cramped quarters, of how firm his square shoulders felt against hers.

"Afraid so. Let's talk about something more pleasant."

Jessica tilted her head. "Such as…the auction?"

"Such as your adorable daughter." He laughed. "Surely you don't think I'd refer to the bachelor auction as pleasant."

"It's going to be fun. You get to meet someone new, and it won't cost you anything. What's wrong with that?"

"I don't like being set up. And this screams of trouble."

Amy mumbled quietly, and Jessica saw her bear on the floor. "It's too far, sweetie, I can't reach it. I'll get it when we stop." Jessica settled back into the seat, wondering if Sam could overlook her past enough to ask her on a real date. "I understand how you feel. A few friends are determined to find me the perfect husband, and the results have been atrocious. I'd just as soon stay single the rest of my life if they are examples of today's average single man."

"And you think I should be excited to throw myself out in the public eye for this kind of scrutiny?"

She laughed. "You're a brave and courageous servant of the community. I'm sure you can handle one date."

"I don't see you putting yourself up for sale."

Amy made a noise that sounded like a sick horse.

"If there had been any men on the committee, maybe they would have suggested we include bachelorettes, too."

Amy said something again, a little louder.

"That's a poor excuse." Sam teased. "What's Amy saying?"

"She wants to see the man on the horse. You know, the statue of the founder of Colorado Springs. You don't have to…"

Sam turned toward the life-size statue of General William Palmer in the middle of the intersection at Nevada and Platte. Amy clapped. "She knew right where we were. That's amazing."

"And what's your excuse? You didn't even know what the fund-raiser was until Adam and Kate's engagement party. Your mother is even helping. You could've given her suggestions."

He didn't say a word.

"So maybe you'd like to serve on the next committee?"

"To help raise money to educate victims about domestic abuse?'' He didn't even pause to think about it. ''Sure. With the increase of domestic abuse, it's long past time we do something. With all of the statistics and research available, I'll never understand why anyone stays in an abusive relationship.''

Jessica couldn't respond. He had asked her time and again after the accident how she got the bruise on the left side of her face. Something about it didn't fit with her other injuries. She hadn't told him the truth then, and she wouldn't now.

Sam drove to the restaurant, a renovated firehouse in Manitou Springs, a quiet little town built into the tight valley of the rocky mountains. ''I thought this might be an easier place to talk. It's not nearly as busy as restaurants in the city.'' Inside, the owner greeted Sam by name, and he in turn introduced Jessica and Amy.

Jessica took the opportunity to make a professional contact, giving her title at the shelter. ''We hold fundraisers throughout the year to support the education and counseling of victims of domestic abuse.'' She explained how the shelter operated and started to go into their mission.

''I'm familiar with the shelter, and their mission,'' the gentleman said. ''I'll do more than a gift certificate. I'd like to make a donation.''

Jessica couldn't hold back her surprise. ''Thank you, we would appreciate any support you could offer.'' She handed him her business card with a promise to include him on the list of donors at the bachelor auction.

Jessica perused the former firehouse. She showed Amy the play area including a child-size fire engine, and introduced her to the two children at the Lego table. While she and Sam waited for a table to open up, they watched the kids play. The two other children were obviously friends, as they chattered together, trying to get Amy to talk.

Sam tipped his head to ask the question quietly. "Does she talk to the other children at her child-care center?"

"Not really. I've asked her pediatrician about it, but he's not concerned. She was quiet before the accident, and it didn't get better afterward. She's an observer. She interacts. She just doesn't talk much."

"Does she talk to you at home?"

"Of course she does." She couldn't help the defensive tone that accompanied her answer. "She's simply shy."

"I didn't mean to upset you."

Sam looked tired and she felt bad for snapping at him. "I'm sorry, too," she said with a wry smile. "It's just that I feel guilty for leaving her at the center. It's hard not to, when child care is one of the benefits. I thought it would be nice to have her close to me all day. With the money saved, I'm almost ready to start looking for our own house. I wonder sometimes if the turnover of children with so many residents coming and going is good for her, or if a small setting, like a family child-care home, would be better. Yet Deanne gives her so much love and attention, I can't ignore that either. Even I can't give Amy as much as I'd like to, after fighting back pain all day." She looked up and realized that Sam was patiently listening to her. "I wish you'd stop me when I carry on like that."

"I've never met anyone who can say so many words in one breath. Besides, it gives me a chance to know more about you."

Jessica felt a small pang of disappointment. "Maybe I'd like to know something about you." Something besides the fact he had no understanding of living with domestic abuse or the challenges of being a single mother.

"Sam, your table is ready." The hostess collected two menus and a children's packet from the conductor's booth.

"Amy, come on, we're going to eat now." Jessica took her little girl's hand, aware of Sam following them. He had some nerve judging her. She recalled all too clearly the days when she'd felt as if she could never overcome the challenges ahead of her. That feeling of incompetence flooded her now.

The table had the privacy and ambience that she'd want if Sam hadn't made her feel as if she couldn't do anything right.

Sam lifted Amy into the booster seat and set the packet in front of her. She grabbed the crayon and whispered to Jessica.

"Can you tell Sam what color that is, Amy?"

She held the crayon up and smiled.

Sam chuckled. "I love the color red. Can you color me a picture?" Then, as if sensing Jessica's annoyance, he cleared his throat and wiped the smile from his face.

Jessica stared at the open menu, trying to hide her inner misery from his probing stare. Her throat tightened and her heart squeezed as she realized she actually cared what Sam thought of her. She wanted to prove to him that the victim he'd met so long ago was strong enough to help other women in the same situation.

Sam reached his hand out to touch hers. "Jessica, I wasn't criticizing. Mom says I was born a detective. I never learned when to quit asking questions. I'm sorry."

She bristled. It unnerved her that he'd known the instant things changed between them. "Am I that easy to read?" Had she been this transparent the last time he'd questioned her, after the accident?

"Not always." He opened the menu and did a good job of acting interested in what it had to say.

She found her standard Caesar salad with chicken, and Amy's favorite, chicken strips. As soon as they placed their orders, Jessica pulled out her file of donations for the auction.

"Jessica." His voice lost that impersonal, professional tone, and she was in no condition to deal with anything personal right now. "Could we start over?"

"Don't, Sam. Let's get on with business." She had a critical fund-raiser to finalize, and back surgery on top of that. She didn't need to take an emotional step back sixteen months. "We have several restaurants left to select from…" She thumbed through the businesses who had donated dining packages, tortured by the look of interest in his gaze.

"Ma'am, could I get you something to drink?" The cocktail waitress waited while she looked through the wine list and menu of fancy well-drinks, tempted to fall back to the crutch she'd once depended on to get through difficult situations with Tim.

"What do you want, Jessica?" Sam looked impatiently at her.

"Do you have cranberry juice?"

The woman seemed annoyed. "Yes, we do."

"I'd like that with a splash of orange juice and a spritz of seltzer. And could I get a glass of chocolate milk for Amy?"

"Certainly." The waitress looked at Sam.

"Whichever cola you have, and plenty of refills. Thanks."

"Oh, Amy, you can't color these." Jessica grabbed the gift certificates from her, relieved to discover that she'd only colored on one. "Here, can you color the dog on the fire engine? See the dalmatian? Just like in the movie—"

Sam interrupted her. "I think dinner at The Ore Cart sounds nice. I hear it's a great place to take a date."

Jessica flipped through the stack again, annoyed to think he'd chosen The Ore Cart because Amy had colored the certificate. "You don't have to take that one, Sam. I'm sure they will replace it. It's only a piece of paper."

"I like it just the way it is. Don't exchange it." His eyes danced with hers, only hers were tripping all over the place.

Jessica didn't know how to take him, as the cynical cop he'd claimed to be this morning, or the charming suitor that he seemed to be tonight.

The waitress dropped off their drinks and a basket of bread.

"Fine. What kind of entertainment would you like? We have a few athletic packages—rock climbing, skiing…" She thumbed through the briefcase. Not finding what she needed, she lifted the bag to her lap and continued searching.

Amy reached for the rolls and knocked over her milk.

"Oopsie," Amy said, wide-eyed.

"Oh, honey…" Jessica grabbed her files and set the entire bag on the ground, then righted the empty cup.

"Waitress, could we get a rag?" Sam gathered napkins and stopped the milk from going toward Jessica's bag, then moved the condiments and silverware into a pile, ignoring the flow of chocolate heading toward him.

Jessica tried to dam the stream with her hand, but it

quickly flowed around it and onto Sam's khaki pants. She closed her eyes, willing this accident to disappear.

The waitress arrived with a clean dish towel ten seconds too late. Sam thanked her, then quickly wiped Jessica's hand. "Accidents happen. This one's pretty minor, don't let it upset you." After he let her hand go, he wiped up the table and then the floor. Their meal arrived, along with another glass of milk. "Why don't we stop by my house for a few minutes after dinner and discuss the date?"

"Date? What date?" Jessica certainly didn't want to chance disaster again during dinner, but she didn't want to go by his house either. She could just imagine what Amy would find to get into in unfamiliar surroundings.

Sam looked at her as if she'd lost her mind. "For the bachelor auction."

"Oh, right. If you need to stop and change clothes, that's fine, but I think a certain someone would do better if I put her to bed before we get the brochures out again. Maybe you could come into my apartment for a few minutes when you drop us off."

"Sounds fine. Amy, how are your chicken strips?"

Amy looked up at Sam, opened her eyes wide and smiled. "Mmm..." She reached for her glass, which was less full this time, but just a bit out of her reach. Her tiny fingers repeatedly touched her thumbs like a clamp, her "word" for "some." Jessica helped her with a drink, wishing she'd exchanged her briefcase for Amy's diaper bag after all. So much for proving her success as a working mother.

They chatted about their childhoods, and Sam was surprised to discover Jessica had grown up in Italy, where her parents were teachers for the Department of Defense.

''I have family in Italy,'' he said. ''Dad met Mom in Rome.''

She smiled for what seemed like the first time since they had gotten out of the pickup. ''I know. Your mom and I have talked about it. Small world, isn't it?''

Sam nodded. ''And getting smaller every day. So how did you end up in Colorado?''

''I met Tim in Italy. He was stationed there after basic training. What can I say, Italy's a romantic country. When he left, I followed him.''

''You just left? How old were you?'' Sam took a drink of his soda and set the empty glass on the corner of the table.

''We were old enough to elope. I told my parents and came back to the States. I was swept off my feet. I landed a couple of years ago.''

''How's that?'' With a crayon in one hand, he outlined a tree for Amy and encouraged her to color it. Amy pulled out a green crayon and colored the trunk and leaves all the same color. He drew a teddy bear and asked her what color bears are. Amy pulled a brown crayon from the bag. She seemed to like playing with Sam.

Jessica, on the other hand, wasn't so sure. She liked him, no doubt. But they were so different. She saw her parents once a year, and he managed to visit with his daily.

She looked up from her salad and into the depths of his brown eyes when he asked, ''What do you mean you landed?''

Jessica stirred her salad while considering how much to tell him. ''Life was different in Italy. Everyone has a glass of wine with dinner. No one thought anything about it. When we got back here, everything changed.

Tim liked to get together with friends when he was home. I hadn't realized how much we drank until we started planning to get pregnant and I quit drinking completely.''

"Unless my math is off, or you mean a second baby, two years ago your pregnancy was long over."

"And so was the honeymoon. I finally put my foot down—" Jessica stopped herself. She hadn't meant to tell him any more than necessary, and here she was airing all of her dirty laundry. She pushed her plate forward after barely eating half.

"Could I bring you any dessert?" the waitress asked, eyeing first Sam, then Jessica. When she saw Jessica's red eyes, she looked back at Sam, as if he'd done something to cause them. "Are you okay, ma'am? Can I get you anything?"

"I'm fine, just recalling a bad day. No dessert, thanks."

Sam answered without a second thought. "I think Amy and I need your peach pie à la mode, please."

"Sam, she's going to take all night to get to sleep after all that sugar."

He smiled at her then, and Jessica knew she was in trouble. The tables had turned since their first introduction. She'd wanted something from him that night, but now, it looked as if he had his own plan in mind.

"Kids go wild from sugar? I thought I read research has disproved that theory."

"Researchers didn't test Amy. And honestly, I don't have the energy to stay up with her tonight. That chocolate milk pushed her limit."

He caught the waitress's attention and changed his order, asking for a bowl of fresh Colorado peaches for Amy, instead.

"Think she'll buy it?"

Sam's sly expression turned her heart to mush. He was a dangerous man. "Probably not, but it was very nice of you to try."

The pie and dish of peaches arrived, and Amy devoured them before Sam had two bites eaten. Amy reached her fingers across the table and again pinched her fingers and thumb together.

"One bite, Mom?" he whispered to Jessica.

"Only if you're willing to keep her busy later," she threatened.

"Not a problem. Amy, say 'please,' and I'll give you a bite."

She motioned "some" with her fingers.

Sam backed away. "No, say 'please.'"

Jessica held up her hand. "Sam..."

"Say 'please'..."

"That's not a good idea, Sam." Jessica tried to warn him, but it took even less time than usual for Amy to lose her patience and pitch a royal fit. "Amy, no."

Sam looked terrified of what he'd done and started to give her the bite anyway. "I'm sorry."

Jessica held out her hand and blocked the spoon with the bite on it. "Don't reward negative behavior, Sam. No matter how desperately you want her to quiet down. Finish your pie and we'll meet you outside."

She dropped a few bills onto the table, lifted Amy and her bag and made a beeline for the exit. Amy kicked and screamed all the way to the pickup, where Sam met them minutes later.

"I'm so sorry, Jessica."

"Amy has no patience. It's not your fault."

Amy lifted her head from Jessica's shoulder and reached out her dainty hand. "Pwease," she sobbed.

"It's all gone, sweetie." He opened both hands to show her, and Amy dove into them. "Whoa, got her."

Jessica let go and winced in pain.

"Are you okay?"

She nodded while her eyes filled with tears. Sam quickly helped Amy into her car seat, then made his way around the pickup.

"By the way, here's your money. I didn't expect you to pay. I invited you out tonight."

"Invited me?" He had considered this a real date? She couldn't think about that now—her back was beginning to burn. She motioned to the truck. "I think I'm going to need help...maybe I could stretch out in the back seat."

He tilted her chin. "I know you're upset, and I heard your back pop, but the last thing you need tonight is to have the rescue unit using the jaws of life to get you out of there." He waited until she mouthed *okay* before he picked her up and set her onto the leather seat, helping her slide to the middle. "I bet you're wishing we'd brought your car now."

She got nervous even when a police officer drove behind her. She couldn't imagine having had to drive with one in the seat next to her. Especially Sam. "Right now, I'm very glad you're here."

"Why don't we take you to the hospital and let a doctor check it out?"

"There's nothing more they can do. I have surgery on Thursday. That's the soonest they can get me in. Just take us home and I'll get ice on it."

"Will you at least let me stay and help until Amy's asleep?"

Jessica took a deep breath and let it out very carefully. "But you have to go back to work."

"That can wait. You need help now."

Chapter Five

Sam seemed to be hitting every red light in town. The good part of that was that Amy had fallen asleep. The bad side was, Jessica's back had her cringing in her seat belt. "Don't you have pain pills you can take?"

"Not until I get Amy to sleep. The medicine knocks me out."

"Don't worry, I'll take care of her." The light changed and Sam hurried through the college campus, then turned the corner to Jessica's house.

"Amy..." Jessica let the excuse drop when she looked at Amy, her head drooping in the car seat.

"...is asleep," Sam finished for her. "I'll carry her in to her bed and come back to help you."

"I'll be fine," Jessica argued.

"What kind of louse do you take me for? I'm not leaving you in this condition."

"I don't think you're any such thing. I don't want to be a bother."

"She's three, I'm thirty-two. It's no bother to get her

into bed so you can take care of yourself, especially when I should really be taking you to the hospital.''

Jessica shook her head in exasperation. ''You think you know everything. Children just aren't that predictable.'' The pickup filled with silence. ''If you're staying, you should park around back in the driveway. I'd hate for you to get a parking ticket.''

Sam laughed. ''Not a chance.'' Despite his remark, he followed her directions to the back alley and shut off the engine. Sam immediately walked to the passenger door and took Amy into his arms. ''How difficult can getting one child to bed be?''

''I have but one regret.'' Jessica turned to him, a look of delirium quickly taking over her eyes.

''And what's that?'' Sam asked.

The corner of her rosy lips turned up. ''That I won't be awake to see this.''

Surely she was joking, trying to make him feel incompetent. Jessica handed Sam the keys to her apartment. ''Go ahead and take Amy inside and lay her on her bed. She'll be awake soon enough to change clothes.'' Jessica moved gingerly to get out of the truck.

''If you'll just wait, I'll help you.'' Sam turned to Jessica. ''What can I do?''

Jessica declined his offer, insisting she'd make her way.

''Leave your bags, I'll come back for them.''

Sam climbed the stairs to the apartment. While Amy wasn't big for her age, he couldn't imagine Jessica carrying her daughter up these stairs. He walked through the tiny kitchen and headed for what appeared to be a bedroom, startled to find a twin bed in what looked nothing like a little girl's room. He turned the corner to the other bedroom, comforted to find another twin bed, toy box, and a pile of dolls. After laying Amy on the bed, Sam pulled her shoes off and Amy pulled her bear to her chest. His niece came to mind, though Natalie and Amy looked nothing alike. Travis's daughter had brought an unbelievable amount of joy to his family's life. It had been Natalie that made Sam realize how much he wanted kids.

He was about to head back to help Jessica when Amy woke. "Day-ee."

Sam stopped and turned toward Amy. *Maybe Dayee is the bear's name.* He had the family bug bad, he knew, but imagining little girls calling him "Daddy" was a bit much.

Jessica walked into the apartment. "Mommy's here, Amy. Let's find your pj's and get you into bed."

"DaDa." There was no dispute now. He'd clearly heard "DaDa." Amy reached for Sam, and his heart swelled.

"I'll help her, Jessica. Where are her pajamas?" He lifted Amy into his arms and she rested her head on his shoulder.

He could see Jessica's agony. Not only was she suffering physical pain from her back, but emotionally, it had to hurt hearing her daughter call him "Daddy." "She's sleepy. She doesn't know what she's saying."

"Right."

Jessica's expression puzzled him. The look was almost contentment. But with the pain, how could that be?

"I thought Dayee might be her bear's name. Or Baby?"

"No…" She set her bags on the table. Jessica shook her head, winced, and let out a deep groan. "It's not."

He wanted to know what was going through her

mind. Was she upset with him? With Amy? Or was she simply in such agony that she didn't feel at all like talking?

"It looks like you found her room. Amy's pj's are in the top drawer of her dresser." Jessica walked stiffly to the refrigerator and removed an old-fashioned hot-water bottle from the freezer. As if she could read his mind, she held it up. "It freezes flat."

"Good idea." He walked past the bathroom and stopped. "Does Amy still wear a diaper? I'm not too familiar with exact ages on that sort of thing."

A faint smile teased Jessica's lips. "Ah, how refreshing, you aren't an expert on everything. No, she'll need to go potty. She's pretty self-sufficient, but I'll get her cleaned up and change her clothes."

Sam wanted to relieve her of duty but realized Jessica didn't know him very well and backed off. "Sounds good."

He watched her hobble past him, and then left Amy with Jessica while he went in search of pajamas. The multicolored dresser coordinated with the curtains and had a Winnie-the-Pooh theme. Jessica handed him a warm washcloth when they returned a few minutes later.

"She washed her hands, but wouldn't let me near her face. Maybe you can work your charm on her."

Amy hopped onto the bed as if the catnap had recharged her battery.

"Jessica…" He wanted to take her into his arms and put the mishaps of the evening into perspective. He wanted another chance. That surprised him, after his initial impression of her.

She paused, clearly annoyed and not in the mood to discuss anything. "Never mind, we'll talk later."

"Yeah, we need to finish talking about your date."

"Our date," he corrected.

Jessica looked him in the eye. "I'm talking about the auction."

He shrugged. "The only way I can stand to think of it is if you're my date." Where he kept coming up with these ideas he wasn't sure, but he couldn't argue with them. He didn't want to see anyone else. Not until he was certain about these feelings for Jessica.

She didn't seem too pleased with his idea. "I don't mean this to sound as harsh as it will, but don't count on it. Not that I wouldn't like to…date, mind you, but the point of this is to raise money. And on my budget…" She looked around the apartment. "I'm saving for a house."

"I see."

"And besides that, I don't think it would look good for the organizer to wind up with the 'prime property'— excuse the analogy, my brain's a little foggy right now." She raised her eyebrows, revealing beautiful gray eyes and a sense of humor.

He liked the gleam in her eye when she called him that, though, as a man of God, he probably shouldn't. "It's nice to know you have high ethics."

"Yeah, now that you understand I'm a clean-cut woman, where are my drugs?" She disappeared, stifling another groan.

Sam heard the rattle of pills in thin plastic bottles, such as a prescription would come in. She returned from the kitchen with a glass of ice water and a hopeful look of relief.

"Thanks for staying, Sam. If you'd just lock the back door when you leave, Amy will come to my room if she wakes." Jessica went into Amy's room. "'Night, sweetie. Be a good girl for Sam."

"'Night, Mommy. Owie better." They blew kisses, obviously both used to the limitations of Jessica's back problems.

Sam noticed that Amy had dressed herself as he and Jessica were talking, even though her pajamas were on backward. "C'mon, Day-ee."

"I'll talk to you later, then," he said with uncertainty as he heard the latch of her bedroom door click between them.

Sam helped Amy onto her bed, then spread his hand wide under the washcloth. "I'm gonna get you," he teased.

Amy giggled and pushed her hand against his, collapsing onto the mattress.

He let her win a couple of times, then made contact and washed the leftover ketchup from her cheeks. "All cleaned up and ready for bed."

He covered Amy with the sheet and turned out the light. "'Night, 'night."

Amy waved to him and he waved back.

He looked around the tiny living room, wondering if Jessica was out for the night. He found the remote control, sat on the overstuffed sofa and turned to the local news.

Tonight, as they were eating, he had realized Jessica had been in party-girl mode with the men he'd seen her with at the Stagecoach Café. She had been far from flirtatious with him. Gut instinct told him the woman he'd spent the last few hours with was the real Jessica Mathers. He knew enough of her past to understand her struggles. Like her temptation to have a cocktail with dinner. Alcohol was a tough habit to break, and he admired Jessica's determination to improve her life one step at a time.

Sam heard toys rattling in Amy's room. "Amy?"

Karumpf. Sam would never forget the sound of tiny bodies jumping into bed. He shouldn't—he and his brothers did the same almost every night growing up. Usually they were pulling some prank on their younger sister, Lucia. The memories brought a smile.

Sam crossed the compact living room to Amy's door, and found her totally immersed under the covers with the corners of a book jabbing into the sheet. She was chattering away in gibberish. He watched for a moment, comforted to see Amy acting like a normal little girl. After the accident, he'd prayed that she wouldn't suffer any problems as a result of being thrown from the car.

He knelt next to the bed. "Could I read the book to you?"

Amy scrambled beneath the sheet, emerging with eyes wide and a smile to match. She nodded.

He opened the book. "If you give a moose a muffin.." He turned to her and frowned. "A moose?"

She giggled and snuggled closer. Sam felt as if his heart had been handcuffed to these two females.

After two books, she jumped out of the bed.

"Where are you going, Miss Priss?"

She giggled, covering her mouth with her tiny hand. "Potty," she whispered.

"Okay, potty is allowed. Then back to bed. To sleep this time."

"Weed anofer book?"

"No more books, Amy. You need to go to sleep."

She stomped as loudly as her bare little feet could muster on the carpeted floor. He heard her flush the toilet and step up on the tiny chair to wash her hands, then stomp back to her bed. She patted her pillow, silently inviting Sam to join her.

"'Night, 'night?"

"Just for a minute." He leaned against the headboard and closed his eyes, opening them every few minutes to check on Amy. He was half afraid that if he closed them for long, he'd never wake up. Soon he felt her tiny fingers rub his whiskery chin. The movement slowed to a relaxing rhythm and eventually stopped altogether.

Sam returned to the living room, surprised to find a very groggy woman waiting.

"How's your back?"

"So-so. I appreciate you staying to watch Amy. I couldn't have managed her tonight." Jessica propped herself against the small round kitchen table.

"I enjoyed it. Being with her reminds me of being with Travis's daughter."

Jessica yawned midsentence. "He has a daughter?" She blinked wearily and her body shifted slightly.

Sam moved closer, just in case she collapsed. "He did. She and her mother were killed in a boating accident several years ago."

Jessica swayed, as if half drunk. "Oh, that's awful."

"I think you'd better get back into bed before you fall and hurt yourself more." Sam offered a hand, and she pushed it away.

"We needed to finish our date." She touched her finger to her lip, contemplating what she'd said. "Talking about it...for the auction, I mean."

"That can wait until tomorrow."

Her eyelids closed in slow motion. She shook her head. "Hnt-unh," she grunted a minute later.

Sam took her by the arm and led her back to the bedroom. "To bed with you."

"Nope, no sleepover bed."

He looked at the twin bed and laughed. "Did you take another dose of your painkiller?"

"Mus...kle relaxants. Feeling much better."

"Good. Now go to bed." Sam helped her onto the bed and smiled. This woman had high business ethics and no "sleepover" bed. He'd been totally wrong about her. Thank God, because he wasn't sure how he'd explain this to Him otherwise.

Sam looked in on both of them an hour later. Amy was sprawled across her bed, and Jessica had carefully propped herself against the frozen hot-water bottle. He had enjoyed the evening, despite the chaos. And he'd unexpectedly enjoyed getting to know Jessica. He reminded himself that she had once had a drinking problem. Nonetheless, she'd made a difficult choice to change her life and had stuck to it, even though it had cost her dearly. Despite the reminder that drinking problems were a lifelong battle, he felt those cuffs tighten another notch.

Sam locked the door and descended the steep stairs. He just couldn't imagine trying to manage them with a toddler and a bad back. It pleased him that she was looking ahead to a home of her own. Hopefully the next one wouldn't have stairs.

He stopped in at the station and checked his machine for messages. An envelope had arrived from the photo lab while he was gone. He opened it and studied the images, which sent him instantly back into that jail cell. Sam dropped into his chair and leaned his head back, studying the crime scene.

Valenti lay facedown on the floor, as if whatever had

killed him had hit fast. Heart attack? Poison? Lethal injection? Or had he taken his own life, fearing the battle that lay ahead? Sam had checked with the infirmary to see what drugs they stocked and if any had come up missing. They claimed they had to check their inventory and couldn't have any definite information to him until tomorrow morning. There didn't seem to be any sign of struggle. No bruising or scratches. The cell had smelled like Valenti hadn't showered since they'd locked him up four days ago.

Sam slid the pictures back into the envelope and pulled a file from his briefcase. He cross-referenced each prisoner on the list with the type of crime he was incarcerated for, then placed them in a stack according to who had been near Valenti's cell at the time of death. Morrelli was in for petty theft and had last seen him in the exercise yard after lunch. He claimed Valenti seemed as normal as he ever had.

Fredricks was in for aggravated burglary, awaiting trial. No history of drug use and his weapon of choice was a sawed-off shotgun.

Sam thumbed through the stack and stopped at Zapata. An illegal alien arrested for drug trafficking. No weapon. No altercations since he'd been locked up, awaiting extradition back to Venezuela. Last saw Valenti at lunch. Sam tapped his finger on the desk, then tossed Zapata's card aside. Drugs. Sat with Valenti at lunch. Venezuela. Could be the link.

Chapter Six

Jessica woke in the morning with a lapse of memory. She had no recollection of hearing Sam leave. The thought frightened her. Had Amy tried to wake her in the night? Jessica's bedroom door was opened slightly, just as she'd left it.

She rolled out of bed and staggered from the pain in the sciatic nerve. She rounded the corner to Amy's room, relieved to find her child still sleeping peacefully with her precious teddy bear tucked under her head. If Jessica hurried, she'd have time to get herself ready before Amy woke. Thankfully, Jessica had bathed Amy before they'd gone to dinner with Sam. With any luck, she'd feel well enough to give Amy another before the surgery.

On her way to the galley kitchen to make coffee, Jessica found the throw pillows scrunched along the arm of the sofa with an indentation from Sam's head. How recently had he left? Had Sam really believed she thought he was being a louse? Far from it. Sam Vance had the makings of a true gentleman. It puzzled her that he had shown any interest in her. After all, she didn't have a squeaky-clean past.

She started her four-cup coffeepot and slipped two frozen quiches into the toaster oven for breakfast. A note on the table caught her attention. Tears formed as she read Sam's note outlining his "dream date." She closed her eyes, wondering how things had gone with Amy after Jessica had fallen asleep.

Jessica showered carefully and dressed, deciding she and Amy would walk to the shelter. It would be easier on her back than getting Amy in and out of her car seat. It was a nice day, and the exercise would be good for both of them.

Large oak and pine trees lined the streets, offering a shaded walk. She would miss the quaint downtown neighborhood when they moved, though the rough part of town was edging closer and closer to her apartment. There was a good reason it was so affordable. The town house she planned to bid on meant a twenty-mile commute, but would also mean giving Amy a real home, something convenience couldn't replace.

She moussed her hair and left it to dry naturally, which wouldn't take long with the temperature in the eighties already. Though she hadn't minded going curly to avoid the pain from styling her hair, she looked forward to letting it grow longer and straight again. Jessica stretched, careful to avoid the hot spots of pain in her back.

"Hi, Mommy."

Jessica turned. "Morning, Sunshine." She knelt carefully to hug Amy, placing a hand on the door frame for support. "How are you this morning?" Jessica reached for Amy's hairbrush.

Amy's pigtails were unevenly frayed, the ribbons

barely hanging onto the baby-fine hair. "Happy. Where's Day-ee?"

Jessica cringed. So, she hadn't been imagining that part of the previous evening. "You mean Sam?"

Amy nodded. "Where's him?"

"Sam is probably on his way to his job. And we need to get going to the shelter. Do you want to play with your friends today?" Amy rubbed her eyes, nodding as Jessica led the way to Amy's bedroom. This morning she wasn't up to explaining to Amy that Sam wasn't her daddy, nor would he ever be.

Jessica was puzzled to find Amy's baby-doll pajamas had been put on backward, then remembered how proud Amy had been to do it herself. Thinking about Sam Vance taking care of her daughter, Jessica felt uncommonly at ease, something as foreign to her as life without pain. Sam seemed to enjoy children. Though she'd been annoyed at the time, she was impressed with how much he knew about raising kids. If and when she married again, a good father would have to be a top priority. Amy obviously knew what a daddy was, and that she wanted one of her own.

Three out of the four men she'd considered dating since her husband's death wanted nothing to do with children. The other had joint custody of five kids, and claimed he wanted more. He was a junior executive of a law firm, but Jessica was less than tempted to date any man when it included mothering a "yours, mine, and ours" family of such magnitude, no matter his prestige. She had just started her life over, along with a rewarding career. She wasn't ready to give it all up for full-time motherhood to a hockey team in the making.

But when it came to Sam Vance, she wasn't so sure. He seemed too... She thought awhile, trying to find just the right word to describe him. Too…sure of himself. Not only did he have good looks and intelligence, but he was a cop and a member of the church choir. She couldn't have much less in common with any man. While she owed him a debt of gratitude for saving Amy from the cold and snowy field that night, his investigation had also left her in fear that she'd lose Amy for something her husband did.

And, as if she needed any other reasons to avoid a relationship with Sam, all she had to imagine was him standing in front of the sanctuary, singing. The last time she'd been inside a church was nearly a decade ago, and the only reason she'd gone then was to make her parents quit bugging her. Even after she'd married Tim, the only times she'd turned to God, He hadn't listened.

"Nope, I don't need someone else nagging me to go to church," she whispered. Too bad, she thought. Sam's kisses were almost enough to get her to change her mind.

After brushing Amy's teeth, they walked to the shelter and greeted the security officer as he opened the gates. Jessica walked past the colorful quilt in the common room, hoping one day to have time to admire the hours the artist had put into it. She checked Amy into the child-care room. The lead teacher, Deanne Jones, greeted each child, making sure everyone signed in.

"Good morning, Amy. How are you and Barney today?" Deanne teased, while Amy giggled. "His name's not Barney either? What could your bear's name be?" Deanne had asked Jessica to leave the secret between them, hoping the precious bear might be the catalyst to Amy opening up. Two months later, the game continued.

Jessica hung Amy's backpack on her hook and completed the check-in sheet. "I have to hand it to you, Deanne, you have the patience of a saint."

"One of these days she's going to talk up a storm." Deanne lifted Amy into her arms and snuggled her the way Jessica longed to do. "How was dinner last night?"

Jessica held on to the hope that a month from now, she'd be the one holding her daughter. "If I were feeling better, even I might get a laugh out of the disasters."

"Plural?"

Jessica nodded carefully. "Oh, Amy was a pill. Sam asked her to say please and she had a tantrum. I picked her up and took her to the truck, and threw my back out completely this time. I think the disk has finally ruptured. I woke this morning with little recollection of last night, but it's slowly coming back to me."

"Only two more days and it'll all be over with."

They talked for a few more minutes before Jessica made her way next door to the administrative offices. For a change, Jessica was relieved not to meet up with anyone.

Jessica turned the computer on and sat down gingerly, gathering information for the auction. It didn't take more than a few minutes to realize that sitting was not going to work. Though she had hoped to avoid it, Jessica picked up the phone and called the doctor. His nurse took a message and agreed to have him return her call right away.

In the meantime, she stacked books on her desk and placed the computer keyboard on top of it. Flipping through her notes, Jessica reviewed plans for the bachelor auction, gaining excitement for the first fund-raising event for the shelter. Donations had been so generous that she already had a jump-start for future events.

Susan, the spunky director, stepped into the room, looking at Jessica as if she were standing on her head. "What are you doing, girl?"

"Oh, hi. I didn't hear you come in." Jessica wanted to get this done, just in case the doctor changed the schedule. "I'm finishing my notes on the auction for Colleen Montgomery. She agreed to run a feature. I've included a short bio on our bachelors, a picture, and a little blurb about their dream dates. We have a meeting this afternoon to set up the publicity, which she'll run the week before the event. Any last-minute requests?"

"As usual, you're on top of everything. But I was referring to the interesting desk arrangement, not your work status." Susan placed a hand on her hip. "Your back must be getting worse."

Jessica explained what had happened during dinner. "I'm in no hurry to see Sam Vance again."

"What a shame. Lidia will be so disappointed. She had such delicious dreams for the two of you." Susan waggled her eyebrows.

"I'm sure Lidia can find her son a more suitable date." Jessica felt her face warm simply thinking of how one thing after another had gone wrong. She'd been so embarrassed by the time they got to her apartment, she couldn't wait to take her medicine, hoping that when she woke this morning it would seem like a nightmare rather than reality.

Susan swiped her hand through the air, dismissing the subject. "Would you like me to find you a different chair?"

Jessica shook her head. "No, thanks. Unless this is a problem…"

Susan laughed, her springy hair bobbing. "It's fine with me, but you look miserable." She wrinkled her brow and gave Jessica an "I don't believe you" glare.

"I am, but I've called the doctor. I'm sure he'll tell me that he can't do anything until Thursday, as scheduled." Pain shot into her arm and through her right leg and Jessica reached for the desk to balance herself.

Susan's face showed her concern. "Surely he doesn't recommend you stand up all day!" With one hand on her hip and her head tipped, Susan may as well be scolding her six-year-old daughters.

Jessica laughed. "That look may scare the stuffing out of the twins, but it won't work on me. I need to finish this and get it to Colleen."

"I will call her myself and reschedule if necessary. You are to get home and into bed, you understand?" Susan pointed her finger at Jessica.

Jessica laughed despite the pain. She had enjoyed getting to know Susan. "Yes, ma'am."

"That's better, Miss Jessica," Susan teased. "I'll bring Amy over after work, along with something for supper. What sounds good—pizza, burgers, Chinese…"

"Why don't I order something to be delivered? You'll have your hands full with the girls, and I'm tired of feeling like a charity case. I'll buy. No arguments."

Susan smiled sympathetically. "One extra child is nothing to a mother of twins, Jessica, but if it will make you feel better to buy dinner, okay." She and Susan settled on a menu for supper.

"Thanks, Susan." Jessica appreciated Susan's continued trust and support. She hadn't had the energy to argue with Sam about the dinner bill the night before, but she would make sure to return the favor somehow.

For the past sixteen months she'd been on the receiving end. She wanted not only to be self-sufficient again, but to give back what others had given her. Her job at Galilee Women's Shelter was only the start.

Jessica found the missing folder of attractions that she'd needed to review with Sam. She looked at his note again.

> Morning at the zoo, afternoon fishing and/or hiking, picnic in the mountains, drive home, drop Amy off at my parents, then a quiet dinner for two at The Ore Cart…as soon as your back feels better…no need to wait for the auction…I'll call you later to see how you're doing. Sam

Jessica set the note aside. After last night, she wasn't sure she could even face him again, especially for an entire day with Amy. That was a long way off anyway, after recovery from surgery.

Jessica pulled her attention back to work. She guessed he must like the mountains, and chose an outdoor excursion package for him and an undisclosed date guaranteed *not* to be Jessica Mathers. Jessica finished the outline and stopped by the children's room. She peeked inside so as not to get Amy's attention. The last thing she needed today was an upset child.

Amy was watching the other children arguing over the kitchen and backed away. Deanne looked up long enough for Jessica to catch her attention, then said, "Chelsea and Zach, time-out! I'll be right back to deal with you." She stepped out of the room to visit with Jessica.

"Susan has ordered me to get to bed. She'll bring

Amy to my house when she picks Hannah and Sarah up after work.''

''Don't worry about her, she's in loving hands. If the doctor needs to move your surgery, just let me know. I'm available.''

''Thanks. Call if you need anything,'' Jessica whispered. ''Have a good day.''

Jessica walked home, frightened by the amount of pain she was feeling. She called the doctor again, disappointed to discover he would be in surgery all day. By the time she had explained the situation to the nurse, she could barely stand.

''The doctor is booked today, Jessica. Take a muscle relaxant and put ice on it. I'll call you back in a couple hours to see how it's doing.''

Jessica did as instructed, and didn't wake until almost five. By then the nurse was frantic. ''The doctor wants to see you tomorrow morning.'' Jessica was instructed to eat a light dinner and nothing after midnight, just in case they went in for surgery right away.

Jessica called Deanne and changed their arrangements, then ordered Chinese food, which arrived right after Susan and the children. While they ate, Jessica voiced her fear of something going wrong. ''If something happens—'' Jessica handed Susan a sealed envelope ''—my parents live in Italy, so my brother would be the first to get here—''

''Nothing is going to happen, Jessica.'' Susan tried to hand the envelope back.

''Hang on to it, just in case. You can return it after I'm home.'' She forced a smile.

Susan set her hands in her lap, keeping the envelope. ''I'm only keeping this so you'll relax. Let's say a prayer.'' Susan offered her hand. ''Girls, come help me

ask God to take care of Jessica tomorrow and allow this
surgery to heal her back.''

Jessica didn't know how to respond. She'd never had
anyone pray specifically for her before. She hated to tell
Susan that beckoning God's protection on her behalf
was a waste of time. It wasn't that she didn't believe
He answered prayers. It was simply that He didn't answer *her* prayers. God hadn't kept Tim from drinking
or getting out of control. He hadn't saved Tim when
that final moment came. And she didn't expect to ever
be fully cured of her pain.

Chapter Seven

Sam stopped at his parents' house, wishing he could make it an early night. After staying so late at Jessica's and continuing the investigation after her emergency, he was exhausted. "Smells wonderful in here. What's the occasion?" Sam sniffed the garlic and seasonings of not one, but several of his favorite meals.

"I'm just making a few meals to take to Jessica Mathers when she comes home from the hospital."

His mother explained Jessica's surgery in full detail, as if she thought Sam didn't remember. "All of this is for her?"

Lidia lifted a pot from the gas stove and poured pasta into a colander in the sink. "Well…yes. I've done them in lunch- or dinner-size portions so she won't have to worry about preparing meals for a while. Jessica seems to think she'll be able to do anything the instant this surgery is over. I have news for her…"

Mom continued to lecture, which made Sam laugh. Most people would take one meal to a family. Only his mother would stock the freezer for a month. "I didn't know you and Jessica are that close."

Lidia smiled. "I didn't know you cared. Yes, I admire Jessica very much. She's a darling woman." Her brows furrowed. "If only I could get her to come to church. I think she'd like Good Shepherd, don't you?"

"It's a little hard to say, because I'm biased. I think everyone should like my choice of church." He hadn't realized Jessica didn't attend somewhere. Maybe he'd misunderstood his mom. But far be it from him to ask her to clarify.

"What did you think of Jessica?"

Sam leaned over the stove and took a spoonful of her special marinara sauce, catching a glimpse into the dining room where the mahogany table had been converted to a pasta-drying factory. Strings of pasta dangled from the wooden racks with fans blowing so they would dry faster. "You even made fresh ravioli and angel hair pasta?" He stood straight, casually draping his arm around his mother's shoulders. "Do I smell chicken cacciatore?"

"Tsk, tsk." His mother shooed him away with her wooden spoon. "This is for Jessica. You are not going to sweet-talk me into giving you her meals."

"Aw, come on, there's enough food here to feed the entire family. There's no way she and Amy can eat all of this alone!"

"You know Amy, too?"

Sam was busted. "I was the first on scene at their accident. Jessica reminded me of her daughter when you introduced us at the Broadmoor." He hoped that satisfied her curiosity.

Max walked into the kitchen. "Evening, Sam. You have choir practice tonight?" His mother turned to kiss his dad, and Sam reached for the spoon. Her small but mighty hand slapped his away.

Sam felt the agony of defeat. "Yeah, at seven." Before his dad had retired, Sam could have sweet-talked his mother into fixing him a ten-course dinner if he'd been so inclined. Now that Dad was home for good, Mom wasn't so free with her time. Sam couldn't be happier than to see them both enjoying one another's company. The entire family had worried about how they would adjust to his retirement. Sam checked his watch. "So what's new with you, Dad?"

"I learned to make pasta, after thirty-five years of marriage to this Italian goddess." His dad nuzzled his mother as if they were newlyweds.

"Thirty-*seven* years," Lidia interjected. "It's your father's fault we have so much extra."

Sam laughed. "Maybe I'd better make sure it's safe to give a sick woman." He reached for the ravioli, not totally surprised by the wooden spoon that loomed over the tray.

"Maybe you'd like to deliver it to Jessica one evening?"

He shook his head and groaned. "Don't you ever give up? I'm thirty-two, you don't have to find me dates like I'm a shy high school kid."

His mother turned off the stove and wiped her hands on her apron. "There's nothing wrong with being shy, Sammy. You have a heart of gold."

"Jessica is the brunette your mother introduced you to at Adam's engagement party, in case you've forgotten her already," his dad added.

"A Vance never forgets."

"That's a relief." His dad smiled. "At your age, you

shouldn't be letting a good-looking lady like her get away.''

Sam gave up and laughed. ''At my age? I have news for you, Dad...'' Sam thought better than to argue with his dad. Maxwell Vance didn't give up on any case, whether it be finding a terrorist network or finding spouses for his children.

''What's this big news?'' Max's bushy eyebrows lifted.

Sam shook his head. His dad may be retired, but he didn't look a day over forty. And Sam still respected and looked up to him as much now as he had when he was ten. ''When I find the right woman, I'll get married. Not until then. Wherever she is, she's worth waiting for.''

Sam had left messages on Jessica's voice mail at work and at home. She still hadn't called him back, but the director of the shelter had assured him she was among the living. He could only presume the attraction wasn't mutual and that Jessica didn't want to see him again.

His dad squeezed Sam's shoulder. ''That she is, son. That she is.''

Sam looked at the foil pans lined up along the tiled counter. Some were already covered, sealed and labeled.

''If you wouldn't mind, could you take these to the freezer for me?'' His mother stacked containers on a cookie sheet and handed it to him.

''You're serious?'' He looked longingly at his mother's chicken cacciatore simmering in the pan and licked his lips.

''I certainly am.'' She looked at the pendulum clock and jumped. ''Goodness, where did the day go? You need to get to choir, and we haven't even eaten. Max, get the tuna salad from the refrigerator. Sam—''

"Tuna salad? With all of this…'' Sam turned around.

His dad pointed toward the garage. "The freezer is that way.''

Sam lifted the tray and headed to the deep freeze.

His father's voice met him at the door. "We counted those.''

"Not even I could eat ten meals of chicken cacciatore in one week, but I wouldn't mind trying,'' he muttered. He closed the door to the garage behind him, planning which night he could let his mother con him into delivering a meal. She didn't need to know he and Jessica had already gone on one date. He didn't want to get their hopes up. Why his father was so antsy for Sam and his siblings to get married after missing eighty percent of their childhoods, Sam couldn't fathom. But he wasn't about to invite any conversation about his own love life.

While they ate supper together, Sam dodged his mother's repeated inquiries about the bachelor auction and Jessica Mathers.

Instead, he steered the conversation to the frustrations of work. "I noticed you talking to Alistair Barclay the other night, Dad. What do you know about him?''

Max chuckled and the lines of his forehead creased. "If you can imagine, he thinks he's going to run for mayor.''

"Are you keeping an eye on him?''

Dad shook his head. "Why? Do you think I should?''

Sam couldn't believe his own father was playing ignorant. He was still trying to crack his father's "undercover'' code. It seemed hopeless. The man had been in the CIA for nearly forty years. The fact he was Sam's father didn't mean Sam would ever understand him.

Sam took a bite of his tuna sandwich, hoping the extra time would make his dad think Sam had information he wanted. "Nothing concrete." He took another serving of cucumbers and onions. "Just a hunch. There's something odd about him. He keeps unusual company, unconventional business hours, and he's moving awfully fast with these buildings."

"Something illegal about efficiency these days?" His dad frowned, leaning back in the captain's chair. "No, you'll have to come up with something more concrete than that. He's created jobs and helped the city come out of this recession pretty well compared to many cities. A lot of people are impressed with that alone."

Sam looked at his dad in disbelief. "El Rey Construction brought in their own people, and a lot of problems along with them. The Narc Unit is adding three officers, hoping to get a handle on calls. Domestic abuse has filled every shelter available."

"Don't get me wrong, Sam. I'm not defending him. Be patient. Keep watching. One day he'll make a mistake, and you'll be there waiting." His dad took another bite and looked at his watch.

Sam took a deep breath and a long drink of iced tea. "You sure you're not working again?" His dad had a sparkle in his eye that had more to do with his love of adventure than the love of his life. Sam knew his mother had come to terms with that decades ago.

Max rested his elbows on the table and folded his hands in front of him. "You know better than to ask. What I can tell you is to trust the gut instinct that God gave you."

Sam understood now, especially when he saw the

look in his mother's eyes. "I'm not an agent, Dad, and if I were ever to consider it, I'd do it like you did, restricting work to out-of-town cases to keep the family out of danger. I guess what concerns me is that you're at home now," Sam said as he looked at his dad. "And Mom deserves this retirement as much as you do." He pushed the chair from the table, kissed his mother's cheek and patted his dad's shoulder. "Thanks for dinner." Sam carried his dishes to the kitchen and loaded them into the dishwasher.

"You coming over for the Rockies game tomorrow night?" his dad hollered as Sam opened the back door.

Sam smiled. "Wouldn't miss it for the world. Love you guys."

"Love you, Sammy," his parents said in unison.

Sam entered the side door of the church, ready to forget the problems of the world for the next couple of hours. He relished this time to focus on God and glorifying Him. Even if people came in the door with a weight on their shoulders, it was a few hours they could join together and let God lift their burdens.

Sam greeted the others and turned on his keyboard. The Praise Team leader stood and looked around. "While we're waiting on Betsy and Rob, why don't we see if anyone has prayer requests."

The list was bountiful—praises as well as needs. When prayer time came, Sam added Jessica's surgery, Travis's grief, and protection for his brother Peter, from whom the family hadn't heard in nearly three years.

Sam warmed up on the keyboard while waiting for the college kids to arrive. Steve gave an overview of what songs they would sing this Sunday based on Pastor

Gabriel's scheduled sermon. Betsy and Rob ran into the room, apologizing for keeping everyone waiting.

"There's a standoff with police!" Betsy's eyes grew large, and she looked at Sam. "Sorry, I forgot, this is your break from work. There's something happening that we should pray for."

Sam shrugged. "It's okay, Betsy, I always keep the officers in my prayers, but I'll say an extra one tonight. If they need me, they know how to reach me." He released the cell phone from his belt and held it in the air. "Let's pray this stays silent."

Everyone laughed and settled into practice. Sam was more distracted than usual, unable to get his mother's comment about Jessica out of his mind. He wondered if Jessica had ever been involved in the church, or if she'd never been introduced to the Lord.

It was one thing to walk away from Him, another altogether to never have known what one was missing.

Practice wound up for the night and he drove home, wondering how Jessica and Amy were getting along. He glanced at the clock, realizing it was far too late to call, especially the night before her surgery.

He pulled into the garage, eyeing the basketball. He listened to his phone messages while he dialed Travis and locked his gun in the cabinet. "You feel like shooting some baskets before it gets too late?"

His older brother and his German shepherd, Cody, walked the not-quite-two blocks almost as quickly as Sam changed into his grubby shorts and shirt.

The sun had gone down and a breeze blew through Manitou Springs. Sam turned on the porch light and met them outside with a bucket of water for Cody and lemonade for himself and Travis.

Sam passed the ball to Travis. "One-on-one or Horse?"

"I don't know—how bad do you want to lose?" Travis sent up a warning shot. "I'm hot tonight."

"Who isn't?" Sam retrieved the ball and dribbled to the half-court line. "So what's up?"

"I hear we both were conned into that bachelor auction." He stole the ball from Sam and made another shot.

Sam shook his head. "So this is how it's going to be, huh?" He dribbled and jumped, spinning while under the basket. "Two points, and you didn't see it coming."

"Thought I'd give you a chance to warm up. No fun playing alone." Travis took the ball out, and Sam reached in for a steal. "Reach," Travis said, claiming a foul.

Sam took a step back, then rushed the basket and blocked Travis's shot.

"I hear Mom's trying to set you up with Jessica Mathers."

Sam lost his footing, and Travis called him for traveling. He slammed the ball to the ground. "You going to keep distracting me?"

Travis laughed. "All's fair in love and war."

"A Vance never forgets. And you know what they say about paybacks." Sam called time-out and drained his glass of lemonade. Travis removed his shirt, and Sam noticed Natalie's baby ring on the gold chain just as Travis took it off. He stepped inside the front door and set it on the shelf. Sam wondered if Travis would ever recover from the loss.

"Jessica and I had dinner last night to plan the date. I think Mom's got her wires crossed on this one."

"The date was a bomb, huh?" Travis took a swig of his drink and headed back for the court.

"It had a few problems. Actually, I like Jessica, but she has quite a history. Her husband was a drinker, probably abusive, though she won't admit it."

Travis hit the rim, and Sam tipped the rebound into the hoop. "She left him, I presume?"

"He killed himself in that car accident a year or so ago. The one that ejected the baby in the car seat—" Sam stopped, worried that the simple mention of a child would upset Travis.

Travis took the shot, but missed and elbowed Sam for the rebound. "Oh, yeah, I heard about that. What a fluke that fate brought you together again."

Sam interrupted the conversation to call the foul and take his shot from the free-throw line. "That's what Jessica and I thought, but now she hasn't returned my calls. Sounds like she and Mom are getting pretty chummy."

Travis started to respond, but Sam called Travis on another foul and stole the ball. "*Calls,* as in plural?" Travis stole the ball back and missed because he was laughing. "Cody, get Sam, get 'em."

Cody stood at the edge of the grass and tipped his head. He knew better than to get in between them while they were playing basketball. Sam tucked the ball under his arm and collapsed on the grass, playing the "get 'em" game with Cody. Cody growled fiercely as he and Sam wrestled, then backed away when commanded to do so. He stood at attention, guarding Sam.

"Good boy, Cody. Forget the game, let's go inside. Let's get you a snack." Sam liked to reward Cody's control. The German shepherd jumped and yipped as they headed to the house. If the time ever did come when they needed him to attack for real, Sam often wondered if he'd do it.

"I called to make sure she was getting along okay." Sam explained how the date had ended and that she was going in for surgery. "What did you think of her?"

Travis thought a moment. "We met at the Stagecoach, but thankfully it was Mom's day off. Jessica was a little too cheery, if you know what I mean."

"Like the life of the party?" Sam offered. "What did she drink?"

Travis nodded. "Yeah, that's about it. I don't know what she had, she asked for her usual."

Sam disappeared into the kitchen and returned with a towel over his shoulder, a treat for Cody and a bag of frozen grapes. "Which looked like, what?"

"Looked like a glass of wine, maybe. Though it was pretty pale for a red wine, but a little too red for zinfandel, come to think of it. Why?" He poured himself another glass of lemonade and chugged it.

Sam felt better. "I've seen her at the café a lot this month, and she's seemed exactly the same. Kind of like she's flirting. She wasn't like that with me, but we took her daughter, since it was a last-minute suggestion. I didn't figure she'd have time to get a sitter."

A smile flickered on his brother's face, and Travis quickly wiped it away. "She wasn't flirting, but maybe…"

"Maybe what?" Sam snapped too quickly and too defensively for someone who'd gone out with the woman once. Nevertheless, he didn't like to hear doubts, especially when it came to Jessica flirting with other men.

Travis silently called Cody and started scratching his ears.

"Maybe some guys would have taken it personally, if they liked the cheery young type. I'm not the best person to notice that sort of thing. I hardly noticed it when my own wife flirted with me. Used to make her even madder than…never mind."

Sam was surprised by Travis's admission and didn't know what to say. His brother had shocked everyone by returning from college married to his girlfriend's best friend, Allison. They'd never figured it to be a love match, but when Natalie had arrived, they'd had hope the marriage would turn around. Sam leaned his head back on the sweaty towel. "You can't change the past, Trav. But I can't say I'm not happy that you didn't find Jessica as attractive as I do."

"I didn't say she's not attractive, I'm only half dead. She's pretty, but that cheeriness would kill me, even from a sister-in-law—just to warn you." His dark eyebrows lifted mischievously.

"Don't put the cart before the horse. No one mentioned marriage," Sam argued.

"Just calling it like I see it, Sammy. I'm heading home." He stood and crossed the room, leaving Sam in a mild state of shock.

Marriage?

When he realized Travis was at the front door, Sam felt guilty letting him leave. He hadn't responded to Travis's mention of his marriage. Maybe his brother had wanted to talk. Sam just didn't know how to tell Travis to get on with life without hurting him. They had already lost one brother with Peter's disappearance; Sam couldn't stand the thought of alienating the only one he had left.

"Thanks for the game."

Travis nodded. ''Thanks for not pushing. Forget I said anything, would ya?''

''You're outta luck there—a Vance never forgets.'' Sam closed the door, too much on his mind to sleep. He found plenty of chores to keep him busy until he finally gave up and decided it was time to go to bed.

Just as he was dozing off, he had a brilliant idea. ''If Jessica doesn't understand *this* message, we don't stand a chance.''

Chapter Eight

Jessica closed her eyes, shutting out the bright lights and noise of the operating room. She counted backward, eagerly anticipating the day when she could carry her daughter without suffering days of intense pain. "Ten, nine, eight..."

When she woke later in her own hospital room, she didn't remember anything from post-op, yet there were plenty of reminders: machines beeping, an IV pole, rails along the sides of her bed. A nurse checked her blood pressure and smiled.

"Amy here yet?" Jessica's throat and mouth were dry, making her tongue feel double its normal size.

The nurse set a jug of ice water on the tray by Jessica's bed. "No one has been here yet. Is Amy a friend?"

Jessica shook her head. "Daughter." Her eyes drifted closed and she slowly slid back into a world without worries that, no matter how hard she tried, she couldn't pull herself out of. She needed to see Amy, but sleep won.

"Get some rest, Ms. Mathers. I'll be back in a little while." The nurse placed the medication button in Jessica's hand. "This will dispense a dose of morphine through your IV. Press the button anytime you feel pain…"

"'Kay." The drugs made her sleepy, and before she knew it, a couple more hours had passed. The certified nurses' assistant arrived with a dinner tray. Where had the day gone?

"Evening, Ms. Mathers. Can I help open anything for you?"

Jessica forced her eyes open. "Why? Can't I do it myself?" She moved her arms, just to prove to herself that the surgery hadn't left her paralyzed. Doctors had laughed at her cynicism, but now that the surgery was successful, she could finally joke about what could have gone wrong.

"Of course you can, I just thought I'd offer to help."

Jessica opened her red gelatin and smiled. "Is my daughter here yet?" She set the plastic dish on the tray and looked at the clock, ignoring the meal.

"I haven't seen anyone. How old is she?"

"Three."

"What a fun age." The CNA chatted away. "Wouldn't you like to try our tantalizing beef broth, gelatin du jour, or an Italian ice?" She laughed at her own silliness, until she saw Jessica's tears. "Sorry, but you can't imagine how awful it is to bring hospital meals to starving patients. Every now and then I bluff them into enjoying it. Is something wrong?"

Jessica forced a smile. "It's not the food. I've been waiting for Amy to get here."

"I see." She asked about Amy, then promised to stop back in after she'd delivered the rest of her dinner trays.

"Try to eat. That's probably why they're not here yet—they're eating, too."

Jessica sank back into the bed, then reached for the phone and dialed her home number, letting it ring until the answering machine picked up. She dialed Deanne's number with no better result. Thinking that they may have been detained at the shelter, she tried there, too. No answer. She shifted in the bed and looked at the clock, whose hands pointed to the opposite poles. If Deanne got off work on time, they should have left the shelter at four. Now it was after six, and Deanne hadn't even called.

The nurse returned before Jessica had eaten anything. Jessica didn't give her a chance to get two words out. "Any sign of my daughter yet?"

The nurse looked at her watch. "They probably went to eat and lost track of time."

Jessica looked at the clock and nodded.

"Let's try sitting on the edge of the bed. Maybe you'd have an easier time eating that way." After a complicated ordeal of moving one object, then a wire, then another object, Jessica sat upright for a few minutes, then tried walking while the sheets were being changed.

The nurse helped her back into the clean bed, and Jessica collapsed, then pressed the morphine button and dozed again. When she woke and saw nearly two hours had passed, panic set in. Where could they be? Had they been in an accident and no one knew how to reach Jessica? Had Deanne remembered to take Amy's backpack, which included the card with Amy's vital information?

The phone finally rang, and she answered. She heard her parents' voices, clear from Italy.

"We won't keep you, honey," her father said. "We just wanted to make sure the surgery went okay."

Jessica said nothing about Amy. She didn't need to worry them. Not yet, anyway.

The nurse entered again. "Why don't we get you up and go for another walk?"

The last thing Jessica wanted to do right now was move, let alone get out of this bed. "I don't want any setbacks before Amy's visit. Can't we wait?" Deanne had agreed to bring Amy to visit right after her shift at the child-care room. Where could they have gone?

"Not really, Ms. Mathers. The doctor's schedule is quite rigid. If you want to go home tomorrow, we need to get busy." The nurse checked Jessica's vitals and turned to get another gown for her to wear as a robe.

Jessica heard Lidia Vance's sweet voice in the hall. She grabbed the rail and relaxed onto the bed.

"Jessica, how are you feeling?" She could hear Lidia, but couldn't see her because the nurse stood between them.

"Physically, fine," she said, as Lidia came into view, "Deanne was supposed to bring Amy to visit after work, but I can't reach them."

"That's odd." Lidia looked at the clock on the wall. "Would you like me to call for you?"

"If you wouldn't mind, that would be a huge relief. Maybe I'm dialing wrong."

"Ms. Mathers…"

"You don't seem to understand—" Jessica squinted, trying to read the nurse's name tag "—Brittany. I don't know where my daughter is. She's only three."

"I'm sure there's been a misunderst—" the nurse started to say, but Jessica cut her off by pounding her fist on the hospital table.

Her dinner tray jumped, rattling the plastic bowls and silverware left from her meal. "No. Something is *wrong*." Jessica's heart raced and she shook her head. "Maybe she's been in another accident." Suddenly Jessica felt nauseated. "I don't know what's going on, but she's not here, and the caregiver hasn't called." She took a deep breath. "This isn't like Deanne at all. She calls when Amy has a runny nose, just to let me know. Something has to be wrong."

"Calm down, Ms. Mathers."

"No!" Jessica yelled. "Can't you call the police? I just know something's wrong. Please help me find out what's happened to my daughter."

"Miss Mathers, you need to calm down or I'll have to—"

Lidia stepped in, cutting off the nurse this time. "I just called Sam, Jessica. He'll be right over. Nurse, maybe if you come back after we talk with my son? He's a detective with Colorado Springs Police Department. Maybe he can clear this up for Jessica."

The nurse looked at Jessica, then back to the elegant petite woman. "I'll send my supervisor in to see if there's anything more we can do to help ease the situation."

Lidia pushed the hospital table across the room after offering Jessica a drink. "We'll get this all straightened out, Jessica."

Lidia gave Jessica a kiss on the cheek and held her hand. Jessica closed her eyes. She didn't want Lidia to let go. She wanted someone to hug her and tell her this was some sort of nightmare, that she would wake up and Amy would be just fine.

"Sam will be here soon. He'll know what to do," said Lidia.

Oh goody, I can't wait, Jessica thought sarcastically. After their disastrous dinner, she wasn't so sure Sam would show up at all. He'd probably send the surliest officer on the force. "Thank you for coming Lidia, but you didn't need to bother Sam."

"It's no bother. He's a few blocks away, watching a baseball game with Max. I thought of how miserable you must be up here alone, and I decided to see if I could cheer you up with some flowers."

"Flowers?" Jessica glanced to where Lidia pointed and her mouth dropped open. She'd been so relieved to see a kind face, she hadn't noticed any flowers. She looked at the huge bouquet near the door and realized Lidia must have set them down before Jessica saw her.

She noticed another smaller flower arrangement, and another. "Who sent all these arrangements? Good grief. I've been so upset about Amy I haven't noticed any of them."

Lidia chuckled. "I'll read the cards—if you don't mind?"

"Oh, no one would be sending me anything too personal. Go ahead. I need something to take my mind off Amy for a minute."

Lidia read get-well wishes from Susan and the staff at the shelter. Her parents sent their love along with a potted plant. Her brother's family sent an arrangement of wildflowers… Lidia stopped.

"What's wrong?"

Her deep-brown eyes opened wide. "I'm not sure, but I'm guessing you know. This card is an apology, from Sam. What's going on?"

Jessica was as shocked as Lidia to hear Sam had sent flowers—a huge bouquet of burgundy calla lilies that matched the oriental decor in her bedroom. "I don't

know. We had dinner to discuss the auction. It didn't
go well, but he didn't owe me any apology. I told you,
you shouldn't have bothered him.''

"Is there someone you'd rather bother when your
daughter is missing?'' Sam said as he barged into the
room.

Jessica looked at him, surprised to find him gazing
at her tenderly.

"What's going on?'' he asked.

His mother sent him a mixed look of pleasure and
curiosity. She tipped her head toward the flower arrangement. "That's what I've been asking.''

"Mother, not now. I mean with Amy.'' His voice
exuded warmth and concern.

Sam stood next to Jessica's bed as she reviewed everything. "The nurses keep making excuses, that I must
have been asleep when they were here, or...'' she blub-
bered, struggling to regain composure. She wanted to
be strong. Needed to be, for Amy. "Or they've gone to
dinner. It's nine-thirty. Past Amy's bedtime. Something
has to be wrong.'' Jessica shook her head. "Deanne
should have called by now if something came up. I
know she understood that I wanted to see Amy as soon
as possible.'' Jessica's tears let loose and she could
barely breathe.

Lidia brought a washcloth and gently ran it along
Jessica's jaw and neck. "Breathe, Jessica. It's okay.''

"I'm not going to tell you you're imagining things,
Jessica. Are you sure she went to the shelter today?''
Tenderly, his eyes melted into hers as she shook her
head. Sam offered a somber smile. "I'll look into it
right away. What we need you to do is try to stay
calm.''

She took a deep breath, trembling with fear and anger. "Something has happened to Amy! How do you expect me to stay calm?"

Sam took hold of her hands and held them still. "Jessica. You've just been through surgery. I don't blame you for being upset, but you need to relax and let me look into it. I'm going to go make a few calls. I'll be right back. Okay?"

She nodded.

Sam asked several more questions, then left the room.

If Jessica had had any hopes that she might be overreacting, they just faded away. This was real, she knew it.

While Sam was gone, Lidia continued to comfort her. Time stood still. The lights in the hallways dimmed, announcing the end of visiting hours. Lidia didn't budge.

Jessica looked at Lidia. "Where is he? Why isn't he back yet?"

Lidia shrugged. "He'll be back soon."

Sure enough, Sam stepped into the room a few minutes later. His hair was a mess, his face pale. "Deanne and Amy never showed up at the shelter today."

Chapter Nine

Jessica didn't want to believe what Sam had just told her. "She's missing?"

"Technically, we don't know where she is, exactly, so I guess you could say that. However, it could still be a misunderstanding."

"Don't give me that excuse." Jessica shook her head and felt the tears burn her tired eyes. "Don't you ever lie to me. Amy is *my* daughter. *My* responsibility. I have the right to know what's really happening."

"You know as much as we do right now, Jessica. You can't do anything to help Amy except get stronger. I have several officers looking into this—checking hospitals, driving records, everything we can do at this point. We'll have more answers in a while. For now, calm down and rest."

Sam's words stung. Jessica was helpless. Truly unable to take care of her daughter. She closed her eyes, more confused about Samuel Vance at this moment than she ever had been. How could he be so calm? Didn't he understand?

"I can't lose Amy, too. I'd rather die."

"I know what you mean, Jessica, but do not let the nurse hear you say that," Sam warned.

She opened her eyes to look at him, then closed them again.

"I mean it. I know you're frightened. I know it hurts. But if you think you've got problems now... You don't want to go into a seventy-two-hour hold in the psych ward. Understand me?"

Jessica's eyes flew open. She realized he wasn't trying to be mean, he was only trying to look out for her. "I didn't mean it. I'm—"

"Yell at me all you need to, but don't lose it with the hospital staff. I'll be here and I'll get you through this."

The supervising nurse stepped into the room with a hospital security officer. Sam confirmed that the hospital security kept surveillance tapes and arranged to look at them.

The supervisor tried to explain the attending nurse's intentions, that she hadn't meant to be argumentative. Jessica nodded her head in silence, indicating she understood. She didn't want to understand. Her daughter wasn't here, and she didn't need anyone's permission to be upset. She was tired of everyone telling her to calm down.

"After you talk to the police, Jessica, I think it would be best if we give you something mild to help you sleep. We'll wait until you're ready. And if they find Amy, we can be sure she stays here until you wake. Okay?"

Jessica stared across the room. *If* they find her? Suddenly this was becoming worse than real—it was her worst nightmare. She was helpless to move by herself, and she could do nothing to locate her daughter.

"We'll let you know when we're through talking to Jessica." Sam's reply pushed Jessica a little closer to losing control.

Lidia returned to the opposite side of the bed with another cool washcloth. She wiped the tears from Jessica's face. "We're going to find her, Jessica. We won't give up till we have. Maybe Travis could help, Sam."

"I'll call him later. I've called another detective in, Jessica. It's standard procedure. She's with the Missing Persons Unit, and I'm not. It will save time in filing the reports and get everything moving as quickly as possible." He smiled at her, then looked to his mother, the grim truth in his expression.

"Missing? You really think she's—" Jessica felt light-headed "—missing?"

"Well—" He looked a bit panicky himself. "When someone isn't where they're supposed to be..." Sam's voice faded away, as if he, too, were facing reality. "Don't jump to any conclusions yet. When did you last see Amy?"

"She was in bed this morning before I left for the hospital. Deanne agreed to get her ready and take her to the shelter when she went to work at seven this morning." Jessica pulled a couple of tissues from the box and took a long drink of water, hoping to avoid falling apart totally.

"So you saw Amy at what time?" Sam pulled a small tablet from his back jeans pocket, sat in the chair and took notes.

She thought back, trying to be exact. "I had to be here at five-thirty, so it must have been somewhere around four-forty-five to five o'clock. I walked to the hospital, so I left early."

"You walked?" He didn't look pleased. His gaze

lingered on her and she wanted to tell him it wasn't easy, but she'd managed all on her own. So what if it had taken her forty-five minutes to make the ten-minute walk? "Do you know what she was wearing?"

"She was in her pink shorty pajamas, I suppose, but surely Deanne put play clothes on her for the day."

"What is Deanne's full name? For our records."

"Deanne Jones," Jessica said.

The detective arrived, and Sam filled her in on what was going on. "Jessica Mathers, this is Detective Rebecca Hilliard."

"Hi, Mrs. Mathers. I'm with the CSPD Missing Persons Unit." The woman, unlike Sam, wore her badge and gun in plain sight.

"Hi." Looking from Sam to the pretty officer next to him, Jessica realized how awful she must look after surgery and after crying for the last few hours. She pulled her sheet higher, even though she felt warmer by the minute.

"Could we open the window?" Jessica asked.

"They don't open." Sam felt her forehead, then handed the washcloth to his mother to rinse in cold water again. "If you're hot, maybe the nurse should check you. It feels cool in here to me." He looked at the others, who nodded in agreement.

Lidia handed the freshly rinsed cloth to Sam, then left to get the nurse, despite Jessica's refusal.

"I'm fine, I don't want any more medicine. I have to stay awake, for Amy," Jessica said to Sam.

"You may have a fever, or an infection. It doesn't hurt to check it out." Sam tried to reason with her as he reached to place the cool cloth on her neck.

"Speak for yourself." Jessica took the cloth from

Sam and wiped her own face. "You're not the helpless one."

Detective Hilliard asked Sam to fill her in on what he knew so far. He hadn't missed anything, even though Jessica hadn't seen him take that many notes. Sam's phone rang and he left the room while Rebecca continued asking questions.

"Jessica, what do you know about Deanne Jones?"

Jessica wanted to cry, but refused to look helpless in front of the police. Sam had already inferred that she fell short of perfection on the mothering scale. This was one more vote for his argument. "She is the child-care provider at the Galilee Women's Shelter."

"Did she go to work today?" Rebecca asked.

"I don't know, I wasn't there. But according to the phone call Sam made, she didn't. I didn't think to call them, because I didn't get worried until after work hours."

Rebecca's pager beeped. She paused a moment in her questioning to glance at it, then looked up from her notes. "Where is Amy's father?"

Jessica felt the room spin. "He died sixteen months ago."

"I'm sorry, I didn't realize." Rebecca paused to look at Sam as he entered the room.

"She's not at any of the hospitals and Amy's doctor hasn't had any call regarding Amy," Sam announced. The room fell silent.

A few minutes later, Detective Hilliard continued her questioning. "Can you give us a description of Deanne?"

Jessica felt tears sting her eyes and closed them to force the tears away. "She's about five-six, slender, very neat appearance...shoulder-length brown hair, I think. It's curly, and it may have highlights. Brown eyes. She has a large, deep scar on the right side of her face. She wears a lot of makeup to try to cover it.''

"Do you know how she got that?" Sam interrupted.

"I heard that she was burned in a fire. I've never asked."

Rebecca had been taking notes and looked at Jessica. "Any particular shape to the scar?"

Jessica touched the right side of her face. "No, it pretty much covers the entire jaw." When asked what Deanne had been wearing that morning, Jessica couldn't recall anything specific.

The detective continued writing. "We need to know who all may have had contact with Jessica recently."

Jessica listed the people at the shelter, including staff and several residents.

"Has anyone shown extraordinary interest in Amy recently?"

Jessica looked at Sam. "No, several people have shown concern about Amy's not talking, but, no, even that's not out of the ordinary. She's very shy."

Rebecca returned a faint smile. "Has Amy ever wandered away from you or the child-care provider?"

Everything was hitting Jessica at once. "No," she whispered.

"Is she happy at home?"

Jessica gasped for breath. "What are you getting at? Of course she's happy."

"These are standard questions, Jessica. We have to ask them," Sam explained. Anguish showed in his eyes and he crossed his arms over his chest.

"I know this is difficult." Detective Hilliard offered to get Jessica a drink of water before they continued. "How long have you known Deanne?"

"I met her two months ago, when I started working at the shelter full-time."

"Do you know how long Deanne has worked there?" Rebecca's long ponytail trailed over her shoulder when she bent her neck to take notes.

Jessica shook her head, feeling like the neglectful mother that Sam seemed to think she was. Just because she trusted people without checking out their rap sheet didn't mean she was irresponsible. Surely the shelter had checked into all of that before they hired Deanne.

"Have you been around anyone who might have just met Amy recently?" Rebecca paused, and Jessica mentally walked backward through the last few weeks. "A new boyfriend or—"

"Just Sam."

The room became dead quiet. Sam stared at her in disbelief. Lidia looked pleased as punch, and Detective Hilliard stood frozen in astonishment.

Jessica looked at them, growing warmer by the minute. "What did I say wrong?"

The silence lengthened. Finally Sam tried to respond. "You, um…" Sam's words caught in his throat.

"You admitted that Sam's your boyfriend." Lidia's smile left no doubt as to her opinion on the matter.

Jessica's tongue stuck to the roof of her mouth. She reached for her water and choked on the lukewarm liquid. "I *what?* No…" Her eyes widened and she looked at Sam accusingly. "No, I didn't say anything of the sort! What did you ask?"

"I asked about anyone new, such as boyfriends…" Rebecca's words faded.

"I guess I didn't hear that part." Jessica looked at him, then up at the flowers. "We…I don't have a boyfriend, new *or* old."

After another pause, Detective Hilliard asked a few more minor questions, then closed her notebook and promised to get back to them as soon as she could. ''Jessica, I need to confirm that we have your permission to search your residence for evidence related to your missing daughter. I would also like to know if there is a photo we could use to issue an Amber Alert.''

''Of course you have my permission. There are photos in the album on the shelf behind the television, but the most recent is in the frame on my dresser. I took a full roll at the shelter last week. I think that's still on the table by the door.''

''Thank you. I'll get back to you soon.'' Rebecca smiled.

Sam followed the detective out of the room. ''Becky, wait just a minute. About Jessica, we had dinner, it was business,'' he told Becky.

Becky kept walking, but Sam knew she'd never let him live this one down. She had that look on her face.

''Sure thing. That explains why Jessica got so hot after I walked into the room.'' She looked at Sam with laughter in her eyes. ''Whatever is going on between you, it doesn't matter to me. We agreed long ago that we didn't have what it takes to make it.'' Her hazel eyes looked as tired as his felt. ''We made the right decision, Sam. You have my blessing.'' She backed away.

Sam stepped into her path. ''It is a coincidence that we broke up when we did. There was nothing, no one who came between us.''

''It's okay, Sam. Really, it is.'' Becky smiled. ''You are so fun to razz, but not tonight. We have a little girl to find.''

He could tell by the tone of her voice that she was

sincere. "Yeah, let me know what you find. I'll call you after Jessica's asleep."

Becky muttered under her breath. "Why don't you stay here with Jessica and let me know if you hear anything? Whether or not you two are seeing one another, I think she needs your support. I'll call with an update." Then Becky chucked him under the chin in her tomboy sort of way. "You two would have beautiful babies together. The chemistry is obviously there. Seems like God found you the right one this time."

"Not so sure about that, but I'll take it into consideration...after we find Amy."

"Hang in there. We'll find her."

The supervising nurse called Sam from the nurses' desk. "Sam, you have an urgent call."

"Go ahead, I'll be in touch," Becky said as she left.

Sam dreaded walking into the room to face the two women in his life. Especially under these circumstances. He wanted more than anything to hand Jessica good news for once, but there was no use delaying the inevitable. Sam stepped through the door and to her side.

"What now?" Jessica moaned.

"Deanne called in sick this morning. No one thought much about it. The officers confirmed that no one with her description has checked into any of the area hospitals. She hasn't been in any accidents, but no one answers the door at either residence. It's now official. Amy's been listed as a missing child."

Chapter Ten

A few minutes after Detective Hilliard left, the supervising nurse returned.

"I don't want any medicine. I need to be awake in case we hear from Deanne," Jessica argued as the nurse prepared to administer the medicine into her IV.

The nurse paused, looked at Sam, then at his mother. "I know how difficult this is for you, Jessica, but you really need to rest. This will help relax your body so it can heal. We're going to keep a very close eye out for your daughter, and if they come here, we'll make sure to wake you. Trust us. Okay?"

Sam gave up fighting away his own misty eyes. He asked the supervising nurse to postpone the medication for another fifteen minutes so they had a little more time to talk.

"That's fine." She turned and left.

His mother gave Jessica a kiss on the forehead. "I'm going to go get a few things from the house and let Max know what's going on, then I'll be back. Would that help, Jessica?"

Jessica shook her head. "It's late, Lidia, you need to stay home where you can rest."

Sam interrupted. "I'll stay here until Mom's back, then come back later so Mom can go home and rest. Wouldn't you feel better if one of us is here with you?"

Lidia didn't give her a chance to argue. "Of course she would. Anyone would feel the same. It shouldn't take but half an hour to get what I need." She kissed Sam's cheek and smiled before hurrying out the door.

Jessica's teary gaze met his. "I'm sorry for everything, Sam. For this, for my stupid comments at the wrong times, for making terrible things happen every time I'm near you."

"Don't blame yourself. As for your comment, I like the idea of being your boyfriend." He waited for her reply.

"What, there's not enough danger in police work these days—you have to include a woman whose life can only make matters worse?" She smiled weakly. "Thanks for the flowers, but you didn't have to apologize for anything."

"You didn't return my calls—does that mean you're not interested?"

Jessica's gray eyes were darker than usual, and Sam realized he shouldn't be pushing her at a time like this. He was about to tell her to skip answering, but her dreamy gaze startled him.

"No, it doesn't. I didn't think a woman taking strong medications should make important telephone calls, let alone leave messages on answering machines." Jessica's nervous giggle turned to tears. "Maybe when this…is all over, we could try again."

Sam hadn't considered what it might mean for their relationship if they didn't recover Amy. She was right—

they shouldn't move into a relationship until the search had concluded. Still, there was no way he could walk away from this case, even though he could count a handful of reasons why he should.

"Sam?" Jessica looked understandably frightened and alone.

"Yeah?"

She reached her hand to take his. "I can't imagine going through this without you and Lidia. Thank you."

His heart beckoned him to wrap his arms around her and comfort her. His brain warned him to keep his distance, not to complicate circumstances. If God was, in fact, leading him and Jessica together, He'd done so for a reason. Was that so Sam could be her comfort? Her strength? Her protector?

Sam took her hand in his and realized it was pointless to deny his feelings for her. He'd told himself again and again over the past week that falling in love with a victim of a case was unwise. Or was it God's way of bringing them together?

Jessica looked Sam in the eye. "Will you stay until the medication takes effect?" she asked.

Sam hadn't noticed the supervising nurse step into the room. "Sure. I won't leave until my mom gets back, so don't worry. Before you go to sleep—do you have your house keys with you?"

"In the closet. It's the jagged key in my waist pack."

Jessica fought sleep as long as she could, but finally lost the battle.

Sam called Becky as soon as his mother returned. On the way out of the hospital he stopped in at the security office and reviewed the few tapes that included blond children. There was no sign of Amy.

The security guard rewound the last tape. "Could the kidnapper have dyed her hair?"

"They wouldn't have come to the hospital if they had changed their looks. It would ruin their disguise." Sam gave the security officer a description of Amy and his cell number to call if he found anything promising.

Afterward he met Becky at the courthouse, where the judge was to sign the search warrants.

Sam realized they were waiting for two warrants, one for each apartment. "I didn't think we'd need a warrant for Jessica's place—she gave me her keys."

Becky nodded. "Since I didn't have them, I figured it was better to cover all angles. I don't want the judge to disallow any evidence. This suspect isn't walking if I can help it."

"You remembered to include any evidence that might lead us to their current location, right? And pictures for the press."

"Got it covered, Sam. Don't worry, we'll find Amy."

"Deanne has a sixteen-hour lead. She could be out of the country by now." Sam looked impatiently at the judge, who seemed to be taking too long to sign the warrants.

Judge Warren looked right at Sam. "You've pushed the boundary on these."

Becky spoke up, as if to remind the judge and Sam that this was officially her case. "A three-year-old—"

"I'm signing the warrants because of the child's age, but do *not* push any further or I'll disallow your evidence. Timing isn't so critical that it's worth letting a kidnapper go free on a technicality. I'm on call all night, you know. Just let me know if you need another warrant to get more evidence." They both watched him scribble his signature and then shove the papers across the desk.

Sam bit his lip to keep from interrupting—he and Judge Warren had a good working relationship. Sam wondered how much Becky had actually included in the warrant.

"Thank you, sir." She turned and headed toward the door.

"What do you have so far?" Sam opened the door of the courthouse and held it for Becky to exit.

"Found an ex-husband, but we haven't reached him yet."

"Anyone else involved?"

"No evidence of anyone."

Becky opened the car door and paused before getting in. "How did Jessica take the news?"

"She seemed to know before we did. Mother's intuition? She's had a lot of tough breaks, and this isn't easy for her to take alone." Sam shook his head. He wanted to be there for her, but he also wanted to be out there finding Amy.

They met at Deanne's a few minutes later and knocked on the apartment door. Sam looked in the windows while Becky jiggled the doorknob.

"See anything?" she asked.

"Nothing." Sam knocked on the door again. "There's a light on at the neighbor's. See if they might have seen anything."

"Sure. I'll also find out if these are privately owned or rentals. You know the drill. This is a solid wood door. It doesn't look like a fun one to bust down." Becky headed next door. "Why don't you see if there's any way in to the garage?"

Sam headed around back while Becky talked to the neighbors.

Sam put on his leather gloves so as not to disturb any fingerprints they may be able to lift. The side door to the garage was unlocked, and Sam was startled to find a high chair, infant seat and other baby equipment stored along the walls.

He heard Becky's voice a few minutes later. "Sam, we're in!"

He closed the garage and joined Becky inside the sparsely furnished apartment.

"The neighbor has a key to let the movers in next Thursday. Somehow I don't think she gave her two weeks' notice to her employer."

"Did they know where she was moving?" Sam asked.

"Nope." Becky pulled a stack of photos from under the edge of the futon and thumbed through them. "Sam…is this Amy?"

He nodded, then looked at the pictures of Amy at the shelter, playing happily. "Use this one for the Amber Alert. It's a good close-up."

"Can't take photos from here unless they have Jones in them. The warrant specified information to where they might be going. We'll look for a picture of Amy at Jessica's and I'll get another warrant for these."

They continued to look around the apartment, speculating whether Deanne could have an accomplice. Becky called dispatch to get a finger printer to meet her as soon as possible. "Did you find anything?"

"Garage was unlocked. Lots of baby stuff…one of those bouncy seats, high chair…"

"Amy wouldn't need those, would she?"

"No. My guess is Deanne had a child of her own, or planned to have a baby. There were fresh oil spots on the garage floor. Any word on her car? Doesn't look like a new one.''

"Officer Mills is working on that for me. He'll put out an APB. I'm going upstairs, you keep looking around down here.''

Sam set the photos back under the futon and continued to look for clues. He turned on Deanne's computer, hoping she'd made plans to visit family or friends.

"Hey, Becky, did you include the computer in your warrant?''

She closed the closet. "Direct correlation would cover us. Find something?''

"Checking e-mail. Just a minute.'' Sam had hoped she stored her password somewhere on the computer, but didn't have the patience to dig. He called his old friend Jake Montgomery for help. If anyone could get him into the system quickly it would be a computer expert with the FBI.

Sam thanked Jake after asking him to keep Jessica and Amy in his prayers. "If you need anything else, don't hesitate to call, Sam,'' Jake added.

Sam jumped when Becky tapped his shoulder. "How'd you get into her e-mail? Hacking on your new list of hobbies?''

He laughed. "I haven't, just onto her browser. Had a little help from the Feds. Anything upstairs?''

"More pictures of more kids, literature from adoption agencies,'' Becky said. "Wonder if she failed to qualify? Or maybe she didn't have the money to adopt…'' Her voice faded away.

Sam continued to peruse the recently used files on her computer. He clicked on the Web browser and hit "history.'' Adrenaline kicked into high gear when he saw a map site listed. He printed off all of the recently used pages. then looked for a way to get into her mail.

"Finding anything?"

"Nothing solid, but based upon her search of cities, I think we'd better find a picture of Deanne Jones and get it to the airports."

They both searched for more photos, disappointed not to find one of Jones.

"Let's go to Jessica's," Sam suggested.

"What'd you come up with on her computer?"

"Several cities on her Internet map site, but nothing concrete. She's quite diverse, or else she's good at setting up wild-goose chases. I found a couple of possible e-mail contacts in her saved mail. No real names. We'll have to get it to Jake Montgomery to follow up. I think there are enough leads to include the computer on the warrant. Her 'favorites' list includes a couple of adoption agencies, one sperm bank. Looks like she's getting pretty desperate to have a baby."

As soon as a uniformed officer and the finger printer arrived, they left, and Sam led the way to Jessica's place.

When they arrived, Sam looked into Jessica's car as he walked past and noticed that Amy's car seat hadn't been moved.

As they walked up the stairs to Jessica and Amy's apartment Becky reviewed what they knew so far. Sam's mind drifted back to two nights ago, when he'd been here with both Jessica and Amy. Afterward, he had hoped Jessica would call, eager to set up a date. She hadn't, and now he could kick himself for moving so slowly. Maybe if he'd trusted his instinct right after Adam and Kate's party he would have been taking care of Amy today instead of looking for a kidnapping suspect.

"Right now, this is the last place we know Amy was seen, in her pajamas," Becky said while Sam blinked away tears.

He recalled his pleasure in reading to Amy. *Lord, take care of Amy, and help us to find her quickly.* He ran a hand through his thick hair. It was about time for a cut, he thought distractedly.

He used Jessica's key and opened the door, memories rushing back. He hadn't expected to feel so strongly for her.

"I'm going to go ahead and look around," Becky said quietly.

The home had been so alive two nights ago. Now it seemed a lonely place. Suddenly he heard someone on the stairs behind him.

"Excuse me. I'm the owner of this building, Herman Raney. Is there a problem?"

Sam turned around and pulled his badge from his pocket. "Detective Samuel Vance, CSPD. Jessica Mathers reported her daughter missing. Did you see Amy today?"

The man's face turned ashen. "But…oh no, Jessica had surgery today."

"Yes, she did. The woman watching Amy never showed up at the hospital to visit this evening as planned."

"Oh dear, I had a bad feeling when I saw that police car pull up earlier, and then you and this other car pull in." The gentleman leaned over the railing. "Catherine, Amy's been kidnapped. The police need to ask us some questions."

"Oh no!" His wife let out a little cry. "Let me get my robe and I'll be right up."

Sam interviewed the landlord while they waited for his wife to join them. Mrs. Raney arrived just as Becky appeared from the bedrooms, and Sam introduced her to the retired couple.

"When did you see Amy last?" Becky asked.

Mrs. Raney wrung her hands. "Must have been a little before seven."

"Are you sure?" Becky asked.

Catherine Raney nodded. "I changed the sprinklers before the morning show started at seven. That woman loaded a bag and Amy into her car."

Becky jotted down notes. "Can you tell us what Amy was wearing?"

"Oh, she was wearing her watermelon sundress. It's my favorite. It has a green trim, then pink in the middle with little black seeds all over." Mrs. Raney wiped her tears.

"And the woman with Amy?" Becky asked, still taking notes.

"She had on blue pants and a collared T-shirt, I think."

"What color was her top?"

"Striped, blue and tan—horizontal stripes." Mrs. Raney told them how much they were going to miss Jessica and Amy once they moved.

"Where are they moving to?" Sam asked.

"Jessica is putting a bid on a house, I think she said. These stairs are difficult to manage with a little one, especially in the winter, and with her bad back, she shouldn't be lifting Amy at all."

"I imagine they would be," Sam responded, remembering Monday night, and carrying Amy up the stairs.

Becky asked for and received a physical description of the woman, but it wasn't much. "Did you hear any unusual noise from upstairs this morning?"

Mr. and Mrs. Raney looked at one another and shook their heads. "Like what?"

Becky shrugged. "More noise than most mornings, the clunk of luggage, suitcase wheels, anything different."

"With a three-year-old upstairs, there are a few bangs and noises now and then. Nothing seems too unusual anymore."

Sam and Becky thanked the Raneys and went back into the apartment. Sam closed the door behind them, even though it was stiflingly hot. "If she planned a kidnapping, why would she hang around for at least an hour before making her getaway?"

Becky stopped. "It would take some time to get things together. Maybe she waited to call the shelter from here, raise less suspicion," she suggested. She glanced at the counter and the pad of paper on the table. "Think we should dust for prints?"

"It doesn't look like anything has been dug through. We know she was here," Sam pointed out.

"No, nothing seems out of place," Becky agreed. "Wonder if Deanne had been here before and knew where things were? Or maybe she didn't take any of Amy's clothes. Did she baby-sit when you two went out for dinner?"

"No, we had Amy with us, but Amy wasn't with Jessica the night of Adam Montgomery's engagement party. Maybe Deanne watched Amy that night. I'll check on that and let you know."

They found pictures of Amy, and one of Deanne with

Amy at the shelter. "Here you go, the two of them together."

"I'll add these to the Amber Alert. If you find anything else, give me a call."

Sam wondered if anything aside from Amy was missing. He looked in Amy's dresser to see if Deanne had emptied them. Surprisingly, they were as full as they had been a few nights ago. Meaning that other than the one outfit Amy wore, none of her clothing would be recognizable for the search.

After he closed up Jessica's apartment Sam returned to the hospital—again with no news.

Chapter Eleven

Sam walked through the quiet hallways of the hospital. This smell had never been one of his favorite aspects of police work—filling out reports while waiting for accident victims to come to, waiting while drunks' blood alcohol levels were tested, that pungent smell of antiseptic after his squad car had been cleaned out. He hadn't missed that at all after moving to Detective for Vice and Narcotics investigations.

He sneaked into Jessica's room, hoping not to disturb anyone. Lidia looked at him hopefully.

He shook his head and whispered, "Nothing yet. How's Jessica?"

Lidia stood. "She woke once and asked about you. The nurse got her up to walk. She may be able to come home today." Even at four in the morning, Sam could hear the teasing in his mother's voice.

"Maybe they should keep her here, with the kidnapping, the stress…"

His mother shook her head. "She wants to get out so she can look for Amy. Any mother would be the same."

"Which is exactly why she should stay in here where someone can take care of her and leave the searching to the professionals." Sam watched Jessica for a moment, confused by his feelings.

"Try to be compassionate, Sam. Why don't you sit down and rest while Jessica is asleep?"

Lulled by the soft noises of the monitors, Sam dozed in the institutional-style recliner. Jessica stirred, calling for Amy, and Sam felt like someone had kicked him in the gut. He wished he had better news to give her. She looked soft and vulnerable as she came out of her sleep.

"Morning."

Jessica recognized him immediately and pulled herself up in the bed. "Hi. Did you find them?" She looked outside at the pink sunrise. "What time is it?"

"Almost six." Sam looked down and shook his head, not wanting to answer her primary question. "Did Deanne mention to you that she's moving?"

"Deanne? Moving?" Jessica asked, pushing herself to a sitting position. "When? Where?"

"Next week. She left a key with her neighbors to let the movers in to pack and move her. We'll contact them in the morning to see if they have an address for us. I'm guessing it's not local. That could be her destination."

Jessica raised the head of the bed and shifted again with an unconscious grimace of pain. "I can't believe Deanne would do this."

She tapped her tray, staring right at him. "Sam, where do we start looking?"

He took her by the shoulders. "Oh no you don't. You're going to lie back down and rest. The police are doing everything possible for Amy right now."

Jessica stared at him for a moment, worrying her lip

between her teeth. "Deanne really took my little girl? She's really gone?"

Sam pulled his attention away from her lips and looked Jessica in the eyes. She'd known instinctively that something was wrong long before anyone else had thought to suspect. Why was she doubting the facts now? "It looks like it. We wish she'd call with a good explanation. Family emergency, something. We'll know more when we talk to the director of the shelter in the morning."

"Someone is there all night," Jessica said impatiently.

"The officer questioned them while I was here earlier, but the night staff didn't know anything more than that Deanne called in sick this morning. Apparently they took her at her word."

"I can't believe this." Jessica covered her eyes and dropped back into the bed.

Sam stepped closer. "Don't do that, you make me nervous."

Jessica looked at him, wide-eyed innocence. "Don't do what?"

"Fall back against the bed," he growled, feeling an unwelcome sense of protectiveness.

"I'm fine. The fusion is complete. The ruptured disk is cleaned out. Don't worry about me. It's Amy that needs help."

He looked at her skeptically. "I haven't forgotten that, trust me. Just don't push yourself too fast, okay?"

"Kinda bossy, aren't you?"

Sam couldn't tell if she was flirting or serious. "I'm concerned about you. With Amy's situation, I know you're going to be tempted to get moving, but you need to take it easy."

"So you're a doctor now?"

His mother laughed. "I do believe you've met your match, Sammy. It looks like Jessica is feeling better. I'm going to go home, but I'll see you both later."

"Thank you so much for staying here overnight, Lidia. It was very comforting to know you were watching over me." She sat up again, waiting for Lidia to come close enough for a hug.

"I wasn't the only one watching over you, Jessica, and God's watching over Amy, too." His mother offered her hand. "Don't you lean so far—we'll hug later. And remember, we have a room ready for you whenever the doctor releases you."

"Thanks, but—"

Lidia patted Jessica's hand. "Don't make a decision yet, the offer stands. Sam wouldn't dare let you go home alone."

Sam didn't need his mother's prompting; he had no intention of leaving Jessica's side unless his parents were there to make sure she didn't go anywhere. "Have a good day, Mom."

Conversation was awkward for a while after his mother left and Sam felt like the unwanted bodyguard. It worried him that Jessica had moved beyond the shock to the reactive stage.

"What will we do next?" Jessica ran her hand through her wavy brown hair, and Sam noticed she wasn't wearing any rings. He hadn't noticed any the other night at dinner either, come to think of it. Did that mean she was ready to move on after losing her husband?

"*We* won't do anything unless instructed to do so. The police have issued an Amber Alert, Detective Hilliard is looking into Deanne's past, and the investigation won't let up until we find her.''

"Surely you don't expect me to just sit and wait?" The look on her face told Sam she was dead serious.

"If I have to hold you down myself, I will." Sam hoped she didn't push the limits. He didn't want to create more tension between them. "I can understand your frustration, but the fact remains, we don't know where to start looking yet. That's what Becky's investigating."

The day shift had come on duty and a new nurse entered the room to check on Jessica. Sam took advantage of the chance to go downstairs for a bottle of soda with a high dose of caffeine. Two all-nighters in one week was more than he was used to.

By the time Sam returned, several media people had found Jessica's room.

Jessica held her hands in front of her face as a camera flashed. "No, I don't have anything to say right now."

A reporter asked how she had chosen Deanne Jones to take care of her child, and suddenly Sam realized he'd grilled Jessica much the same way. No wonder she'd been offended. Sam tried to push into the room, but Colleen Montgomery had already taken the upper hand.

"Jessica Mathers has just been through surgery. She asked for privacy, and all reporters will leave now. And I'll take that roll of film." Jake's younger sister held out her hand, and the reporter handed her the film, along with sharing a few choice words.

Then the room emptied as if the police chief had just flashed his badge.

Sam laughed as the unauthorized guests fled. "All those years playing cops and robbers with Jake, Brendan and me served you well, Colleen. I couldn't have done it better myself.''

"Hey there, Sammy... I thought this was Becky's case.''

"It is. I'm here to—''

"—make sure I stay out of their way,'' Jessica finished.

Sam looked at Jessica and smiled. "That's not true.''

Colleen glanced from one to the other and smiled softly. "Yeah, I get it. It's personal. I thought I saw you two out on the terrace at Adam's engagement party.''

Jessica turned red and Sam just shook his head. "If you're here in an official capacity, Colleen, I'm going to have to ask you to leave.''

Colleen laughed. "Better watch it, I'm not done writing the feature for the bachelor auction, Sammy. Be nice to me, or I'll have you married off by the end of the month.''

"We could only hope,'' said Susan Carter, laughing as she entered the room.

An uncomfortable hush replaced the laughter as Susan stepped to the side of the bed. "I heard the news this morning and just about fainted, Jessica. I'm so sorry.'' Susan took hold of Jessica's hand and held on to it. "I didn't even question it when I got the message that Amy was sick.''

"It's hard to believe this is happening.''

Sam glanced at his watch. It had been almost twenty-four hours since Deanne had made her move. "I'm glad you're here, Susan. We wanted to talk to you.''

Susan turned. "Sure, whatever I can do to help. I can't believe Deanne could do this. There just has to be some mistake.''

Jessica's eyes watered but she blinked the tears away.

"We keep hoping that, too, but it doesn't look promising. Now we just have to hope Deanne will come to her senses and bring Amy home."

"Susan, obviously you had no clue that Deanne would do anything like this. Who did she report to, and what did she say when she called in yesterday?" Sam took out his notebook and turned the page.

"Deanne left a message with the front desk that Amy wasn't feeling well. I wasn't in yet. Deanne is supposed to be there at seven, and my hours are nine to six. She reports to me. I covered until the other caregiver arrived at eight-thirty."

"Do you know where Deanne was when she called?"

Susan shook her head. "No, but we have caller ID. Maybe it's still on the box."

"Would you call and ask the receptionist not to touch it until an investigator looks at it? And if you have a chance to pull Deanne's personnel file, I'm sure Detective Hilliard will want to look at it as well."

"It's in my office. I'll have it ready."

Sam picked up his cell phone and called Becky to see if the officer had checked for a number on the caller ID box the night before.

"No, but the bank just called in reference to the Amber Alert," Becky informed him. "Deanne came into the bank yesterday morning to get cash. She had Amy with her. They're checking her debit card and will call us if she uses it."

Sam wished he could step into the hall, uncomfortable with the three sets of eyes and ears tuned in to his every word and nuance.

"How much money does she have in her account?" he asked as he turned away from the women.

"Enough to last her a while. She'll have to dip into it sooner than later if she's on the run."

"How much cash did she get? Enough for plane fare?"

"Wouldn't do her any good, she'd have to show her ID. She took eight hundred, so it will last her a while. I put an APB out on her car and have contacted state patrol in the surrounding states as well."

He finished updating Becky and returned his attention to Jessica, careful not to interrupt Susan praying with the other two women. From the doorway Jessica looked terrified—more so than she had through any of his contact with her.

Sam waited until Colleen and Susan left to consider his next step. He closed the door so no one else could walk in and bother them. It was time they had a talk.

Chapter Twelve

"What are you doing?" Jessica watched the door close, then looked at Sam. The fine lines on his forehead seemed to have deepened since their dinner date.

"I don't want any reporters or even friends listening in." Sam closed the gap between the door and the bed, and her heart raced. "I want to make one thing clear, Jessica. I never meant to give you the impression that I felt you weren't a good mother. As I heard the reporters asking you questions, I realized how something so easily said can be misconstrued. I think you misunderstood my questions at dinner the other night."

Jessica wasn't sure what to say. "I'm a little sensitive this week, I guess. I've been so consumed with myself that it's no wonder people are questioning my decisions." She closed her eyes and tears threatened again. "My comments must have made Deanne think she was justified in taking Amy. That she deserved a better mother."

"Why do you say that?" Sam's eyes were filled with

tenderness and compassion, which elicited a war of emotions in Jessica.

She wanted to remember Sam as the cop determined to reveal the problems in her marriage, not as a sensitive, caring man whose presence made her heart pound.

She avoided Sam's gentle gaze before realizing that staring at his broad chest wasn't any wiser. It only made her wish she had someone to protect her and tell her nothing bad would ever happen to her again. No one, not even Samuel Vance, could make that kind of guarantee. Her head swirled with doubts. Should she really tell him? Or would that only make things worse?

"Well? What did you say to Deanne?" Sam's inquisitive voice caught her off guard. She didn't want to face him, yet she had nowhere else to go.

"We were friends, I thought I could trust her and share my frustrations with her. Maybe she misunderstood me." Jessica tugged at the sheet, meticulously straightening and smoothing every inch of it over her legs.

Sam waited, then cleared his throat. "Go on."

"The morning after we went to dinner, I told Deanne that Amy had been a pill." Jessica could hardly think about it, let alone say the words aloud. "I know Amy didn't mean to color on my papers, or spill her milk, and I didn't mean…" The tears won. "I made lots of stupid comments, but I never really meant them. I was tired, and overwhelmed with being a single parent and dealing with this constant pain. I can't go on without Amy." Jessica heard the meal cart rattle past her room and figured her breakfast would be arriving soon. She would almost welcome an interruption to this conversation, although she was too worried about Amy to eat.

"We'll find Amy," Sam insisted. He took hold of

her hand, and Jessica pulled herself up. Sam tentatively placed his other hand behind her shoulder blades to help her. "Careful."

Jessica clicked the button for the pain medicine and waited for it to take the edge off. "How can you be so certain? She's been gone almost twenty-four hours already."

"I have faith."

"And what happens when that fails you?" She already knew the answer to that one; she'd been living with it most of her life.

A hush descended on them as Jessica waited for his answer.

"You pray God will help you adjust, just like He did after your husband died. It wasn't easy, I'm sure, but you're making a happy life for you and Amy."

"I was trying, anyway. Look where that got me."

Sam let go of her and folded his arms across his chest. "You have to believe in order to know the truth."

Jessica shook her head. "I'm not naive enough to believe that I can wish my daughter back and she'll instantly appear."

Sam paced the room. "You're right about that. Bad things happen to everyone, even those who live seemingly perfect lives. But God allows everyone to be tested to see how strong our faith is. To show us His ultimate power." He paused and looked at her. "God wants to answer our prayers. To give us our heart's desire. But we have to believe He can and will do it."

Jessica felt her heart racing. She wanted to believe in God, but every time she asked Him for help, bad things happened anyway. "Why are you so worried about me? I mean, are you just such a nice guy that you take care of everyone this way? Staying on duty all night, begging them to believe in God, praying for their salvation? Or do you feel you have to take care of me because your mother wants you to, or…''

The silence stretched between them, broken only by the muffled clamor in the hallway. ''I think the reason fits into the 'or' category— It might possibly be…'or'—'' He stumbled over his words. He looked down at his feet, then seemed to study the fluids going through the IV. ''It doesn't make much sense…'' He sat on the edge of the hospital bed and turned toward her.

Jessica touched his very handsome unshaven cheek and looked into his cocoa-brown eyes, feeling perfectly at ease. ''What little you know about who I am should send you as far in the other direction as you can run.'' Her hand brushed over his curly dark hair and came to rest behind his shoulder.

''Love defies logic, and in case you didn't notice, I'm not running,'' Sam replied.

Jessica fought to control her swirling emotions. Love? Was he claiming to love her?

She froze, not knowing what to say, then inched closer until her lips touched his. This kiss was as memorable as their first had been, under the romantic lighting at the Broadmoor Hotel, with that familiar element of emotional upheaval. Only this time the kiss was something she'd eagerly anticipated, almost as if it sealed a promise between them.

Jessica pushed herself away. What was she doing, kissing Sam like that when her daughter was missing? She had no business even thinking of romance right now. The notion of a commitment terrified her, especially to a man whose faith was obvious to anyone who could look past his badge. She recalled the day she'd read that article in the *Colorado Springs Sentinel* about the Christian Cop. This man's double trouble, she thought.

Sam stared at her, baffled. "Jessica? What's wrong?"

Jessica didn't have a good record in reading people, and right now she wasn't in any frame of mind to make promises to anyone, especially a detective. She pushed herself from his protective embrace, feeling the warmth of his hands on her arms disappear. "I can't believe I just did that." Pressing her lips together, she awkwardly tugged at the shoulder of her hospital gown to blot her lips. "I'm sorry…"

"Are you okay? Did I hurt you?"

She took a deep breath, shaking her head. "No, I'm just so confused right now." She realized her pain medicine hadn't worked, and clicked the button again, noticing it beeped this time. Maybe she'd pressed the button too soon. She wanted the medicine to numb the pain in her heart as well. "My daughter is missing, and the last thing I should be doing is kissing a cop."

Sam didn't move. "Look at me, Jessica."

She felt a sudden chill and then his hands again covered her bare arms, rubbing gently.

"Please," he whispered.

When she gathered the courage to look up, his eyes were gentle and understanding. Warm and comforting.

"I know this seems sudden, and I don't blame you for feeling confused and frightened—"

"Frightened is an understatement." Jessica felt her pain disappear and the morphine relax her body. Her confidence slipped a notch when she glanced at his strong jaw and full lips. Samuel Vance was as near perfection as any human she'd ever met. "You are the most—" she closed her eyes and turned away, wishing he'd give her some distance, wishing that morphine didn't feel like truth serum right now "—the most intriguing man I've ever met, Sam, but we're so different, and this is a really bad time to start a relationship."

"This started long before Amy's kidnapping, didn't it. Or was I imagining things?" Sam quirked one eyebrow.

"Imagining what, exactly?"

"That you acted totally different when we met at Adam and Kate's engagement party than when you were out with those other men?"

Jessica stared at him, not quite believing her ears. When she'd seen him at the Stagecoach Café, she hadn't even made the connection between the officer that had responded to the accident and the detective she had seen recently. She recalled the Sam Vance who'd responded to her accident. That cop had been arrogant enough to push a grieving woman. It wasn't easy to see this loving side of him.

"How did I act differently?"

"You questioning my observation skills?" His tight-lipped smile oozed with confidence.

She felt her face heat up. "I'm questioning your analysis. I didn't intentionally act any differently with you. And while we're at it, I have a few observations of my own."

"Such as?"

"Oh no you don't, you haven't answered my first question yet. What makes you think I'm interested in you?"

Sam backed away slightly and stared at her as if he didn't like being questioned. She waited patiently, meeting his gaze, despite the fact that she knew her eyes must look terrible from crying.

"You don't put on any fronts with me. With the other guys, you were always smiling, a little too happy..." He paused and looked into her eyes. "At first, I was sure it meant that you hated me, and enjoyed their company. But then—" he cleared his throat "—I realized you were nervous around me. With them, it was part of the sales pitch, so to speak."

Jessica felt her heart beat double time as the truth tumbled from his lips.

"You didn't have a personal investment at stake," he said. "And one isn't normally nervous unless emotion of some kind is involved."

Jessica pulled her lower lip between her teeth. It was frightening to have someone able to read her so precisely. "Okay. So?" *And I'm still nervous around you,* she silently acknowledged. She couldn't even deny his accusations. She may as well have admitted how quickly she'd fallen for him and elevated him to hero status.

"So, you told me never to lie to you," he said calmly.

"I meant with the search for Amy." She'd heard enough truth for today. Sam Vance couldn't be in love with her. And sooner or later, he'd realize it.

The corner of Sam's lip twitched. "*Never* pretty much covers everything in my book. And I want to ask the same of you."

Jessica backed away, a hoarse whisper all she could manage. "There are some things best left in the past, Sam. Things I don't want to talk about."

"You think I'll change my mind about how I feel?"

"Maybe you should." Sam didn't want to know everything about her and she definitely didn't want him to. It seemed like her life had been one poor decision after another. No matter what Sam said, there were some things that were better left in the past.

Surprisingly, Sam didn't seem angry or hurt, just tired. "You had an observation?"

How could she ask such a personal question after refusing to be open with him? "Never mind." She grabbed the rail of the bed and shifted, prompting Sam to move. She pushed the button to raise the head of the bed to support her back, but hit the TV button instead. She fumbled with the control, finally content to mute the sound rather than wait for it to scroll past all the channels to "off" mode.

Through the interruption Sam showed no sign of relenting. "If I can't answer, I'll tell you. Regardless of my promise, there are plenty of questions I flat out can't answer. There are times I'm obligated to reserve the truth until it has to be told. Doesn't change my vow. Trust is one challenge of being involved with a law enforcement officer. I won't ever lie to you. Now, what was your question?"

Sam took her breath away. He surprised her. Everyone described him as strong and silent. This man had just bared his heart to her. She wished she could come up with a different question, but changing the focus of her brain wasn't in her control right now.

"How long were you and Detective Hilliard together? And how long since you broke up?"

His thick eyebrows flinched. His voice was courteous but patronizing. "We dated quite a while."

The truth wasn't quite so easy now, she noticed. "How long is 'quite a while'?"

"Who's the detective here?" Sam smiled, and she relaxed. "A few years. She didn't, and doesn't, want children. I do. The split was very friendly. After all, we have to work together.''

''When?'' Jessica didn't want someone expecting her to pick up the pieces and try to put them back together, because especially right now, she didn't have the strength to do that for anyone. At the same time, she couldn't expect someone else to pick her up and put her back together. Which was exactly why she couldn't fall in love with Sam. He deserved someone who had the strength to support him after a bad day. She wasn't sure she did.

Sam's gaze didn't stray. ''We struggled to stay together for a month or two after your accident. I couldn't get Amy out of my head because she reminded me of my niece, and the fact that Natalie never got another chance to be with her dad. Travis has never been the same. I've prayed every day that you wouldn't have to go through that, too.''

As if he could read the warning signals going off in her head, he continued. ''I came so close to listening to the other officers that night when they told me there wasn't any baby. I couldn't explain, even at the debriefing, why I was so certain that Amy was out there somewhere. About a month later, Becky pushed the issue of kids, and I realized just how determined she was not to bring kids into the world. We've both been much happier since we came to terms with reality. It doesn't work, forcing a relationship between two people who aren't meant to be together.''

''And you think we'd be different? I see my family maybe once a year, and you probably see yours every day or two. I have a past that I can't even talk about, and your life is squeaky clean.'' She looked at him, sad that for once in her life she couldn't accept a nice surprise. "It's clear that I can hardly meet the needs of my daughter and myself, let alone anyone else."

"Everyone has issues now and then." The sun's rays illuminated the entire room, shedding the light on their discussion as well.

"Some more than others. Get real, Sam. You could never—" Love had seemed almost like a dream a while ago, but now, it was the worst nightmare she could imagine. "Face it, I'm hardly the type you'd take to church meetings."

"You think we vote people in and out or something?" Sam backed away. She'd hit a nerve. "We're not so different. Your cup may be half empty, mine's half full. And I haven't met a Christian yet that's perfect."

Jessica turned away. "Look in the mirror."

A quick knock on the door interrupted, and Kate Darling stepped through the door. "I heard you were here, Jessica. I'm so sorry about Amy." Kate placed the blood pressure cuff on Jessica's arm and began the routine check.

"Thanks," Jessica muttered, glancing at Sam, wondering how he'd handle the interruption.

Kate had an odd smile on her face. "Hi, Sam. How are you doing?" She held up a finger, silencing everyone while she released the pressure and watched the dial.

"Good to see you're feeling well enough to be back to work. How's Adam feeling?" Sam's mellow baritone was controlled. It was clear that he didn't want Kate here, but he was far too polite to send her away.

Kate rubbed her shoulder. "We're getting better every day."

"How are the wedding plans coming along?" Jessica

asked, longing for a happier subject as the thermometer was placed in her ear.

"Wonderful, until this happened. I was going to bring the music over this week, Sam," Kate said hesitantly as she placed everything back into the vitals cart. "Do you think you'll still be able to play at the wedding?"

Jessica struggled again with her image of Sam, this time as a musician—a Christian cop who played the piano. She lowered her head and closed her eyes, listening as Kate and Sam discussed the musical selections for the wedding.

"Drop them by my parents' house, Kate. It's closer, and I'll probably be there more than my own house this week."

"Sounds good." She recorded Jessica's vitals, then headed toward the door. "I need to get on with rounds. I'll see you in a while, Jessica."

Sam's voice was calm and his gaze steady, though he stood up and started pacing the room. "As we were discussing, I'm far from perfect. It's probably selfish of me to burden you with my feelings at a time like this."

"You're right about that," she muttered. "I can't think about anything except that Amy is missing, Sam. I just can't." The pain medication hadn't done a thing, and she reached for the button again, except in her confusion, she pressed the call button instead. "See how confused I am?" She yanked on one cord, then another, until she found the right one and pressed it.

"I can see that you're confused. You're even confusing me. I'm sorry if I misread your feelings."

"No, you didn't. It's frightening to see how you know me better than I know myself." She rubbed her eyes and shook her head. "I think they exchanged my painkiller for truth serum. You wouldn't have had anything to do with that, would you?'' She peeked up at Sam, ready for his arrogant smile.

He smoothed the sheet and sat down again, his mouth curved with tenderness. He beckoned her into his arms. ''There's nothing wrong with needing to be held once in a while. And I won't mention this again until you're ready. I'm sorry that I've upset you. I just wanted you to know why I can't walk away from you, or the investigation.''

Sam wrapped her carefully in his embrace. Jessica closed her eyes, her mind spinning in bewilderment. Did he need to be held, or was he, again, reading her mind? ''I hope Deanne is giving Amy lots of hugs. She likes hugs, too,'' she said.

Jessica couldn't recall being held this tenderly since her own childhood. No kisses, no ulterior motives, just comfort from one friend to another.

''I'm falling in love with you, Jessica. And I won't stop looking until we find Amy.''

No, her inner voice screamed, *you can't love me. Not now.*

''Heavenly Father,'' Sam said softly. ''Embrace Jessica and Amy with Your comfort and love until Amy's back home and in our arms. Amen.''

When Jessica opened her eyes she saw Amy's picture on the television and gasped.

Sam jumped away and looked at her. ''What is it?''

She pointed to the television. Sam turned around and his shoulders dropped. ''Turn it up.'' He pulled the cell phone from his belt and dialed a number from memory.

Jessica frantically searched for the mute button on the television, but couldn't find it in time. ''Have they found her? What were they saying?''

Chapter Thirteen

A determined knock on the door preceded the entrance of the surgeon and the nurse, Kate Darling. "Good morning, Jessica." Dr. Reinhart nodded to Sam.

"Morning." Jessica let go of Sam and shifted in the bed, turning her full attention to the doctor. Sam stepped away. "How soon can I go home?"

"That will depend on a lot of factors," he said, looking at her over the rim of his glasses. "I hear you've had a rough night," he said, tucking her file under his arm.

Jessica nodded. "That's for sure."

The surgeon patted her shoulder. "I'm sorry to hear about your daughter. I'll keep both of you in my prayers." He asked Jessica several questions about her level of pain from the surgery and her emotions from the additional stress of the kidnapping.

"I think I'm doing okay, considering." She didn't mention the added factor of a budding romance on top of everything else.

"If you feel like it's getting to be too much, or are

having trouble sleeping, let me know. We can give you something to help. If you'll roll to your side, we'll see how the incision is doing and see if we can consider letting you go home today. That is, as long as you have help." He looked at Sam, and Kate broke into a smile.

"You're aware that the press has already been here hounding Jessica," Sam offered.

Jessica glared at Sam before turning her back to him and the doctor. She had to appear calm and in control or they wouldn't let her go. She had to hold herself together.

"Yes, Detective, I'm aware of that. Unfortunately, if Mrs. Mathers is doing well, we can't justify a longer stay. She'd probably rest as much if not more at home. Jessica, I presume you arranged for someone to help you take care of the wound, cleaning it and so forth, as instructed."

"She has help," Sam answered, before she had a chance to explain that her help had run off with her daughter. "She'll be staying with my parents, Lidia and Maxwell Vance. They've had lots of experience taking care of injuries with four kids."

"Of course, Max is Henry's brother. We were sorry to lose such a talented surgeon as your uncle." He studied Sam a moment, then smiled. "You must be Sam, then. I saw that article in the paper a couple of weeks ago. Keep up the good work, Detective. Come here and I'll show you how to take care of this wound, and you can instruct your mother. Okay, Jessica?" The surgeon touched her arm and leaned over her shoulder. "Okay?" he whispered.

She nodded. What choice did she have? She'd asked Deanne to help her after she returned home, and Deanne had taken Amy. She shuddered.

"We're going to remove the gauze and clean it before we let you leave." He opened Jessica's gown from the neck to her waist and folded the top edge over her arm. He carefully removed the dressing. "Looks good. No sign of infection. Sam, wash your hands and come here so I can show you what to do." She listened as Dr. Reinhart cleaned the wound and explained to Sam what the surgery had entailed. She felt Sam's tentative touch replace the skilled hands of the surgeon.

"How're you doing, Jessica?" the doctor asked.

"Fine."

Kate ripped open the new dressing and dropped the used bandage into the red receptacle. She proceeded to check Jessica's vitals. "Are you sure you have adequate care at home?" Kate asked, and Jessica nodded. Right now, she couldn't think beyond Sam and his family.

Sam asked detailed questions with childlike curiosity.

"Hey, careful back there, you're not going to open it up for a third time, no matter how interesting it sounds."

Sam laughed softly.

She turned her attention back to Kate with an apology. Certain that Lidia would be glad to help, since she'd practically adopted her in recent months, Jessica answered, "Yes, I'm sure Lidia won't mind, and with the kidnapping, Sam wants to stick close in case new information comes in." Though Sam had intervened without her consent, it did make sense, and she would have more freedom and privacy at the Vance house than in the hospital. If she ended up going with Sam to find Amy, he would probably do the wound treatment anyway.

Though she'd had several male nurses over the past

few years, it was different having Sam touching her incision, even with the doctor's instructions.

"Jessica, how's your stomach feeling?"

"Rumbling. Can I eat this morning?"

"We'll try a soft diet. If you have no problems, I'll release you this afternoon."

The doctor sat down and discussed the stress Jessica would be under and reminded her to take it easy. Another nurse popped her head inside the door, "Detective Hilliard is here to talk with Mrs. Mathers."

"Yes, let her in," Jessica ordered, anxious for some news. "We saw something on the television just a few minutes ago. Have you found her?" She could hear raucous voices outside her door. "Who's out there?"

Becky walked around to face her. "No, I'm sorry, we haven't found her. That was the Amber Alert. It's helped having the picture. How are you feeling, Jessica?"

She tried not to sound as cranky as she felt. "Fine, thanks. Who all is outside?"

"The Denver news stations want to talk to you. Along with some rubberneckers hoping to get a glimpse of the distraught mother," Becky said.

Puzzled, Jessica repeated, "Rubberneckers? What are those?"

Sam interjected. "Curiosity seekers. They hear something is happening nearby and they stretch their necks as far as they can to see what's happening."

"Oh."

"Hospital security has been instructed to get them out of here and take the press downstairs to wait for us."

"Why? What have you found out?"

"We haven't found Amy yet, but we're getting response from the Amber Alert already. That's good. As for the news stations, it sometimes helps the kidnapper realize what she's done to see the parents' reaction,'' Becky said quietly. ''You don't have to do it, but we want to try everything we can to help. They want me to give an update on the search efforts, but I wanted you to hear it from me first.''

Jessica's heart raced and her eyes watered: Becky's voice seemed like a faraway one talking to someone else. This wasn't supposed to happen to her; she'd had her share of rotten luck.

''We know that Deanne and Amy were in her bank at seven-thirty, and from what we could see on the surveillance cameras, Amy looked happy and fine. I don't expect that to be any different now. Deanne pulled out a sizable amount of cash, but we calculate she'll have to get more before the week is up, or use a credit card, in which case we can track her that way. We've ordered her phone records, talked to her family in Kansas, and think she took Amy to replace her own daughter who died in a fire almost a year ago now.'' Becky looked at Sam. ''We don't think Amy is in any danger. From what her ex-husband and family tell us, Deanne went into a deep depression when she found out that her daughter died in the fire. Since she took a job as a child-care worker, we believe she equated happiness with being a mother. Sam found a full setup of baby furniture and supplies in her garage.''

Jessica looked over her shoulder at Sam. ''You knew and didn't tell me?''

''Becky is the detective on this case, Jessica. It may have been nothing. I didn't want to upset you with bits and pieces that may not have been relevant.''

''This isn't going to be easy, Jessica. Sam has a personal interest in finding Amy, which means he should step back altogether. But he's human, and an officer, and taking a cop out of a search is like taking chocolate away from a woman.'' She shrugged. ''Unless you object…''

''Not at all. I didn't mean that. I'd like him to stay on the case if he can. He found Amy before, um, after my accident. Maybe he can again.'' Jessica felt her face flush when she realized she sounded like she'd placed Sam on a pedestal. She moistened her lips. ''I understand why he didn't mention it. So what's next?''

''If you feel up to it, talk to the press.'' The detective reviewed the routine questions, and agreed to intervene if the reporters asked anything that Jessica and the police couldn't answer.

Becky talked to the doctor while Jessica apologized to Sam. ''I'm sorry, Sam. I didn't mean to sound so untrusting. I—''

His eyes probed her. ''You're doing great, Jessica. I appreciate your confidence in me, but Becky's trained in missing persons. I'm not. But I do want to be here for you, and if we get a lead on Amy, I won't hesitate to follow it up if Becky can't. I want to tell her the thoughts you had about your comments to Deanne. It may or may not help, but she's the one putting the pieces together—you never know which piece may be vital.''

Suddenly Jessica realized that every part of their conversation would be constantly scrutinized and could end up part of this investigation. She looked at Sam, and he smiled.

''I won't tell any of our personal conversation, in case you're worried. But if finding Amy depended on telling that, too, I trust Becky.''

She felt his strength pass to her and nodded her consent to share their conversations. "I feel as if I can't keep any secrets from you."

"As it should be. And I hope we have the chance to share a lot more secrets." He kissed her forehead and turned to Becky.

Kate helped Jessica out of the bed and wheeled the IV pole into the rest room, then closed the door, leaving Jessica alone for the first time since discovering her daughter was missing.

Jessica took a deep breath and closed her eyes, refusing to give in to depression. She looked into the mirror. It was a miracle Sam hadn't already run the other way. If she was going to speak to the press, she would have to clean up and look strong enough to take care of a rambunctious three-year-old. She turned on the shower and quickly scrubbed her face and hair, keeping her back as dry as possible.

She'd just turned off the water when she heard the anticipated scolding from Kate.

Jessica blotted herself dry. "I'm not going on the news looking so pitiful that everyone will side with the kidnapper."

Kate laughed sympathetically. "Next time, you'll take the dressing off before you shower, then after you're dried off, have Sam put a little ointment on and replace the dressing. I'll be right back."

"Would you get my clothes while you're at it? I've had about enough exposure in this gown for one day."

She heard Kate explaining to Sam and the doctor, "We have a fighter on our hands, gentlemen. She's ready to take on anyone who stands in her way."

Jessica smiled as tears rolled down her face. "Hang in there, Amy. Mommy's coming to get you."

Chapter Fourteen

Later that day Sam escorted Jessica home from the hospital. She'd held up well through the press conference, losing her voice only once in her touching plea for Deanne to bring Amy home. The hospital staff had rallied together to help bolster Jessica's confidence. She looked vulnerable yet strong and determined by the time the cameras rolled. Her hair looked soft and touchable, and with a bit of makeup from the nurses, no one could tell she'd just been through surgery. The burgundy sundress she'd worn gave her a healthy glow, and flowed comfortably over her incision. She fielded questions about her surgery and the ability to get back to a normal life with unbelievable optimism.

Flowers had come in from friends and strangers once the news hit the airwaves, and Jessica had suggested that they be donated to other patients, all except for the calla lilies Sam had given her. She had tucked all of the cards into her overnight bag, hugged the vase to her chest, and said her goodbyes to the staff.

Sam had seen one of the reporters get into a black

car as he went to get his pickup, and called Travis to come run interference if the need arose. It took a little extra coordination, but they managed to lose the car in the Palmer Park area where the streets were narrow and didn't run straight through. There were benefits to knowing all the back roads.

By the time Sam drove into his parents' garage, he'd gone thirty miles out of the way to lose the tabloid journalist.

"Will I be able to go to my apartment today?" Jessica asked.

The look in Jessica's eyes made him wish again that he could make all of this trouble vanish into the thin Rocky Mountain air.

"I really think you should stay here for a while," Sam answered as unselfishly and honestly as he could.

"What if Deanne calls my apartment?"

Sam paused. The medication hadn't affected her thought process. "We'll have your calls forwarded. Do you have a cell phone?"

She shook her head. "I don't have call forwarding either."

"That's easy enough to take care of—"

His dad opened the back door and welcomed Jessica, interrupting the discussion. Sam's mind kept a list of details to tend to as soon as Jessica was settled.

"I'm Max, Lidia's roommate. Come on in."

Sam groaned. "Dad retired recently. He traveled a lot, so he's still getting used to thinking of this as his permanent residence."

Jessica laughed. "Oh, so this is like a second honeymoon."

Lidia rushed through the huge kitchen, catching only

Jessica's comment. "Oh, Sam, you didn't have to tell her that!"

"I didn't say anything, honest." Sam laughed, knowing his parents wouldn't believe him.

His mother was as shocked as Sam. "You two even think alike. I tell you, God has a plan for you both."

"What did I say?" Jessica looked as bewildered as she did tired.

"Honeymoon," Sam whispered. "I always tell them they're as giddy as newlyweds."

Jessica beamed. "How cute. Sam, do you know how lucky you are to have such a happy family?"

"Yeah, I'm blessed." He didn't need to fill her in on the entire truth right away. Not that they were unhappy, just that they were not happy in quite the way the average middle-class family used the term. One brother had been missing for three years, the other had been grieving for fourteen.

Thankfully, he and Lucia had managed to keep the upheaval in their lives to a low rumble, which, considering one worked Vice and Narcotics, and the other had forged her way into the fire department as one of the first female firefighters in the city, was a miracle in itself.

"Most kids wonder if their parents will adjust to both being in the house all day. We were worried how ours would manage living in the same town for more than a week or two at a time. Yeah, I have a lot to be thankful for."

Jessica, still carrying the flowers, looked around for a place to set them.

"Oh, here, let me set those in the dining room." Sam headed into the next room, still talking. "Dad, could you get Jessica a cell phone? We're going to have calls forwarded from her house to it, just in case Deanne calls. I'll call the phone company.''

''I'll take care of that, too,'' Max added.

Jessica reached for a purse that didn't exist. ''Sam, we have to go by my apartment. I don't even have my purse or money…''

''Don't worry about that.'' Sam didn't dare tell her that his dad kept several activated cell phones in the basement for emergency cases such as this.

She continued as if he hadn't spoken. ''And I'll need a change of clothes and other things. And you needed me to see if anything else is missing. I didn't even think of my stash of money.''

Sam lifted an eyebrow. ''Where is it?''

''In an old pair of tennis shoes,'' she said.

He made a face and plugged his nose. ''I doubt Deanne would look there.''

She looked guilty. ''Well, I suggested it at the counseling sessions at the shelter once. The discussion was about fleeing abusive relationships. I shared…what I'd heard once.''

Sam didn't push, though he wanted to. Then again, part of him was afraid to hear her admit it. That was the past, he reminded himself. She's obviously changed. ''Your landlords said reporters have been waiting outside all day. Maybe by morning they'll have given up, and we can run by.''

''I picked up a few things I thought you might need, Jessica,'' said Lidia. ''They're in the guest room. Sam, would you show her where that is? If you'd like to nap before dinner, you'll have plenty of time.''

''Lidia, you're so sweet to share your home with me. You shouldn't have gone to the extra trouble to get me something, too. Thank you.'' Jessica looked at Sam.

"Everything is catching up with me. I didn't think I'd be able to sleep another minute, but it sounds pretty nice right now. Any word on…Amy?"

"No, but I'll call Becky. I'll let you know if anything has changed."

Jessica glanced at him, her gray eyes dull, as if she'd lost hope in finding Amy.

Sam led the way, showing her around the first floor of the house.

"This is a really pretty house, Sam." Jessica seemed overwhelmed with the spaciousness.

"And this is your room," he said finally.

Jessica stepped up to the door, then turned and looked into the bedroom across the hall. "And whose room was this? I take it he liked basketball."

Sam smiled. Jessica was beginning to relax and Sam liked that. "He still does." Sam found himself resisting the urge to kiss her.

Jessica's smile looked sleepy, especially from close up. "It was yours, wasn't it."

Sam couldn't imagine how she'd come to that conclusion. He and Travis both loved basketball. All three boys were in law enforcement somehow, and when they'd all lived here their rooms had never been clean enough to tell one from the other. Of course, now that they were in their own homes, his mother kept the house spotless. He looked into the room and back to Jessica.

"Why do you think it's mine?"

Jessica laughed. "Your mother told me."

"Ha ha." Sam's gaze lingered on her lips, which were beautiful when she smiled. "Why don't you get some rest?"

Jessica raised to her tiptoes and brushed a kiss across his lips. "Thank you, Sam."

She closed the door, and Sam went into his old room and dropped onto the bed. Using his cell, he checked in with Becky and gave her his parents' number to call if anything came up. She had delivered Deanne's computer to FBI computer expert and old friend Jake Montgomery for inspection and was waiting to get reports back from the investigation on her fire.

Sam closed his eyes, said a short prayer, and dreamed of bringing Amy home to her mother—and a father.

Two hours later, Max woke them for dinner, with the surprise news that Sam's sister and brother, Lucia and Travis, had also come to eat with them. Except for the disturbing reason for their gathering, it would have been a monumental way to let Jessica get acquainted with his family. As it was, everyone seemed to walk on eggshells, which wasn't anything new. Anytime Travis was in their parents' home the same chilly atmosphere prevailed.

Jessica's eyes were puffy again. She'd obviously not slept as well as Sam had.

Travis held the chair out for his sister and mother, while Sam doted on Jessica. "Nice to see you again, Jessica."

"Hi, Travis. I was able to make the arrangements you wanted for your auction date."

Travis rolled his eyes as Lucia razzed him. "Hot date, huh, Travis? Who do you think the lucky lady will be? You *are* going to get a haircut, aren't you?"

Travis ignored the baby of the family. "I'm really sorry to hear about Amy. If I can do anything, Sam has my number. I don't like to step on official toes, but then again, I don't care much about red tape anymore either."

"Thanks, Travis. I'm sorry to learn about your daughter, too."

Sam felt the room spin as everyone seemed to gasp at the same time. No one in the family mentioned Natalie or Allison unless Travis initiated the subject.

Travis held himself together. With his usual gruffness, he said, "I hope you don't ever have to find out what it's like. We'll find Amy."

Jessica forced a smile and the tears threatened again. Sam offered his hand, and she accepted, blinking the tears away with determination.

Max blessed the dinner and added a prayer for Amy's safety and Jessica's quick healing, then helped Lidia bring the meal to the dining room. For the next hour, dinner was the main topic of conversation, along with Lucia's latest jokes from the fire station.

The phone rang, and everyone froze. Lidia answered, then handed the phone to Sam.

He wasn't surprised to hear Becky's voice. "What do you have?"

"Nothing more," she said regretfully. "But I'd like to come by and talk to Jessica for a bit."

"Anything specific?" He took the empty water pitcher into the kitchen, using the excuse to get away from listening ears.

Becky hesitated. "I want to discuss some theories."

"Theories? Such as?"

"Why don't I just talk to Jessica about this?"

Sam shook his head. "You tell me what this is about first."

"Come on, Sam. I called as a courtesy. It's not like I don't know where you two are."

"And you know enough to know you're not coming in to ask anything without telling me what you've found. She's already distraught, and I don't want anyone telling her how slim the chances get of finding Amy alive every day she's gone. It's bad enough that I know the facts.'' Sam waited for some lame argument. ''What theories?''

Becky let out a huge sigh, as if knowing he wouldn't give up. She knew him well. ''You should know me better than that. I think replacement is clearly her motive.''

''We came up with that the first search. Is that all you've found after two days?''

Becky never was one to beat around the bush and that she was doing so now scared him. ''Fine, here it is. Could Jessica have said something—'' It sounded like they'd been cut off.

''Becky, what'd you say? You cut out.''

''Could she have given Deanne permission to take Amy? We found comments logged into a journal at the shelter.''

''No, she wouldn't have given up her child. Absolutely not.'' Sam closed his eyes. He couldn't believe anyone could think that of Jessica. Couldn't believe *he'd* ever questioned her parenting.

''Sam, we need to talk to Jessica.''

''Did anyone else in the shelter back up that theory? Did anyone else ever hear Jessica say any such thing?''

''No, but…''

Sam didn't like the way this investigation was going. ''Get over here. And bring the journal.''

They managed to finish eating before Becky arrived. Sam answered the door, and the rest of the family sat down in the living room and waited for Becky to take the first step in the wrong direction. Sam knew that if any one of the Vances had any doubt about how the investigation was being handled, they'd take it into their own hands.

Becky was aware Travis had retired from the force, and had a general idea what his father had done for a living. When she finally asked Jessica about the journal, there was less innuendo than in her phone conversation with Sam.

Jessica's face still turned white. "No, I never…" She swallowed again, trying to gain control. "I would never give my daughter up to anyone. I struggled with having to leave her at a child-care center at all. Having her in the same location was the only way I could deal with it."

"Could you ever have made any comments to give Deanne the impression that you didn't want to be a mother anymore?"

Jessica lost it and the tears wouldn't stop. With her permission, Sam told Becky about Jessica's comments to Deanne. Jessica asked to read the entries, and pointed out that Deanne had outright lied about the day she'd gone home from work and left Amy at the center. "Sam and Susan both can tell you I had no choice. Susan brought Amy to my house after work, not Deanne." Jessica took a deep breath and started shaking. "I can't believe I trusted her with my precious little girl. What are the odds of finding her?"

Sam couldn't believe Jessica had actually asked the question. Thought it, yes, but it was totally different to say it aloud. He looked at Becky.

"If we were looking at a revenge motive, it would look grim, but we're ninety-nine percent positive that Deanne loves Amy and wants another daughter. I don't think Amy's life is in any danger." Becky smiled, then subtly straightened her shoulders. "We have some very good leads with the moving company and the bank. The fact that she didn't close her checking account helped immensely. She'll have to come back to town for more money. I was able to convince the president of the bank to freeze her accounts.''

Sam couldn't believe Becky had accomplished that so soon. "Good job.''

She didn't acknowledge his compliment, which he didn't exactly blame her for. He hadn't been very supportive during their phone conversation.

"Jessica, if you think of anything else that may have anything to do with the case, please call me anytime." She closed the journal. "For the record, we'll get statements from other co-workers regarding Deanne's journal entries. I doubt that we'll need them, but it's better to get them now while these events are fresh in their minds.''

"Thank you, Becky." Jessica stayed seated while Becky stood to leave.

As Max showed Becky to the door, Sam stayed with Jessica.

"I think I'm going to bed now," she said.

Jessica's announcement shocked him. "Let me help you off the sofa." He took her hands and pulled her to her feet. "Are you okay?"

"I take it that's a rhetorical question and you don't really want me to answer it," she said in a melancholy tone.

His mother saved him. "Jessica, could I heat you some chamomile tea to relax you?"

"No thanks, Lidia. I think I'll call my parents to let them know where I am and what's happened, then take my pain medicine. That should put me to sleep. Travis, Lucia, it was nice of you to come tonight."

Lucia hugged Jessica. "You need anything, Jessica, we're here for you." Travis and his dog, Cody, left right after Becky did.

Max returned, and she thanked him for his hospitality, then said, "Good night, Sam."

He crossed his arms over his chest, suppressing the urge to follow her. "'Night."

Sam gave his parents strict orders to call if Jessica woke, then made a quick trip to the precinct to pick up messages and check in on the Valenti case. He'd lost a couple of days' work, and couldn't take a chance of losing more time on that investigation. He stayed about an hour there, then made the ten-minute drive to his house. After picking up a few clean clothes, he would return to watch out for Jessica himself. He pulled into the drive, surprised to find Travis and Cody there.

Travis shot the basket, then moved out of Sam's way. "What's up?" Sam asked as he closed the truck door.

"She's one strong lady," Travis commented. "But she's on the verge of fighting back."

Sam nodded. "Yeah, that's why I'm going to stay at Mom and Dad's. She needs someone on her side to keep her out of harm's way. Nothing hurts more than to watch a woman cry and not be able to help. I wish I could be out there looking for Amy myself, but I think Jessica needs me here with her. I hope she does, anyway."

"Sounds like Becky's doing a good job," Travis said with a grin. "Must be a little awkward."

Sam unlocked the house and went inside. "Not really. I was never really sure it was over, until both Jessica and Becky were in the same room. Becky never really stood a chance."

Travis laughed. "It's about time you realized that."

Sam couldn't believe Travis had never voiced his questions about the relationship before. "Well, since you're in an analytical mood tonight, what's your feeling about Jessica?"

"Don't get defensive," Travis said.

"I'm not, yet. You offered an opinion, I'd like to hear all of it."

"Jessica's strong, but not as aggressive as Becky, if you want a comparison."

"I don't," he said, trying to argue that he'd never made his own comparisons. "A simple approve or disapprove will do, thanks anyway."

Travis laughed. "You don't need my approval."

"Didn't say I did, but you seemed to want to talk."

Travis tossed him the basketball. "It's nice to be needed once in a while."

Sam wasn't sure who his brother was referring to—himself, or Jessica. "No argument…"

"She needs someone who has confidence in her. Someone who can overlook her past and, at the same time, help her find the happiness she deserves. Would you like me to look into Deanne's moving plans in the morning?"

Sam was still back on Travis's idea of the kind of man Jessica deserved. "What?"

"The kidnapper. Thought I'd look into it, if you want. Check with her doctors, see if this could have been avoided." Travis made his way to the kitchen and looked for a snack. "If you have any suggestions, let me know."

"I'd like you to stay out of it for a while, Travis. It's not easy to ask that, but I'm afraid that Deanne might get spooked if she sees the walls closing in around her."

Travis frowned. "I know what you mean. You never

know if the woman is a loose cannon ready to go off.
She's desperate enough to take it this far, who knows
what else she's capable of?''

"I know what you mean. I hate asking you not to do
anything, but I'll let Becky know you're ready to step
in if she needs help. I'd better get going," Sam said,
unable to stop thinking about Jessica. "Why don't we
both get some sleep tonight and talk tomorrow?''

"G'night, Sammy." Travis popped his basketball out
from under Sam's arm and turned toward the door. Then
he grabbed his daughter's baby ring from the shelf
where it'd been since their last basketball match and
slipped it over his head.

Sam checked on Jessica when he returned to his parents' house and fell asleep as soon as his head hit the
pillow, only to be woken a few hours later by the sound
of water running. He listened for a few minutes before
realizing it was Jessica. Jumping from the bed, Sam
looked around for his shirt.

Jessica's door squeaked open, and Sam gave up the
search. At least he'd thought to bring his sweats to sleep
in. He stubbed his toe as he opened the door and
stepped into her path. He hobbled into the hallway and
glanced at her sundress and sandals. She stared at him
with her guilty gaze.

"I'm guessing you're not headed to the kitchen for
a drink of water," he said.

"No, I need to go to my place." She hugged her bag
to her chest and looked away, trying to hide her red
eyes.

"It's the middle of the night." He yawned and
looked at her bedside clock. "You can't just sneak out
of here, Jessica. Number one, we have an alarm system.

Two, you don't have a car. And three, I'm not about to let you walk there at this hour.''

She sniffed and wiped her nose with a tissue, and Sam wrapped his arms around her, relieved when she didn't fight him. She let go of her bag with one hand, hugging him close. ''I need to go, Sam. I just need to.'' Her sweet-smelling hair tickled his bare skin. Her fears wove themselves into his heart and squeezed.

He realized her need didn't come from logic or self-ishness, but from a deep desire to connect in some way with her missing daughter. ''Let me find my shirt and shoes and I'll take you.''

Chapter Fifteen

Jessica couldn't believe how difficult it was to make it up the stairs. How in the world had she managed these for so long, and with a small baby? And it had been only a couple of days since she'd been home.

"How're you doing?" Sam asked.

Was it the dread of facing her house without Amy that made it such a difficult climb? "I'm getting there."

"You don't have to do this, you know."

"Yes." Jessica paused, tempted to back down. "Yes, I do."

"Jessica. We can come back another time."

"No. The reporters are finally gone. I need to do this now, without anyone watching."

"Do you want me to wait outside for you?"

She had thought she wanted to be totally alone, but she realized now that she needed someone to hold her hand. And she wanted Sam to be that someone. "No, I didn't mean that the way it sounded. Well, I did, but I don't." She rolled her eyes, wishing she could just keep blaming the medicine, but she didn't figure that excuse would work much longer.

"I understand either way."

She stood still at the front door, as if bars had locked her out of her apartment. She couldn't imagine their home without Amy's bright smile and throaty giggle. "I can't do this."

Sam wrapped an arm around her waist and helped her put the keys into the lock. "Come on, honey, we can do it. Let's get inside before we draw unwanted attention. You had to get a few things, remember?" He helped coax her inside, then closed the door behind them. "I know this isn't easy, but we can't let Deanne win."

Jessica glanced around at the one place that should have provided her comfort, yet knowing Amy was gone, she felt sick to her stomach. The memories assaulted her, wreaking havoc with her nerves. "I don't know what to do, Sam. I..." She shook her head. "I feel like I did something to cause this. That Amy really does deserve a better mother. I think God is punishing me for all those wild years."

Sam brushed the hair from her face and pressed his lips to her forehead. "No, don't think that way. You didn't do anything to deserve this. Deanne has some serious problems that she didn't deal with. *She's* wrong. No matter what our past mistakes, Jessica, God is a loving God. He's merciful and forgiving."

"Then why is Amy gone? Why haven't we found her?"

"Because something in Deanne snapped. Maybe she lost hope. I'm not sure, but you didn't do anything to deserve this." Sam opened his arms wide and held her tenderly. "We can't lose hope, Jessica. I have faith that we'll find her."

They'd no sooner stepped into her living room than the tears began. Jessica didn't want to be alone, yet she wanted to curl up in Amy's bed and cry. Each step felt like her last. She couldn't imagine how families could live through the loss of a child. She recalled the teenager who had been found almost a year after she had been taken from her bed. Her family had had no choice but to move on with their lives. They had other children. Jessica had only Amy. Without her, what would she do?

"Amy is the reason I had this surgery. So I could be a better mother." She wandered through the small apartment. After Tim's death this had been home to Amy and her. It hadn't been ideal, but they'd managed through the rough times.

"Jessica, you have a message on your answering machine."

Despite logic telling her it wouldn't be Deanne, her heart raced. She reached for the "play" button, but her hand was shaking too much to press it. "It's probably my parents."

Sam brushed his hand through his hair, taming the unruly strand that kept falling onto his forehead. "You called them last night, didn't you?"

"Yeah, but they'd called, before they had my new number," she said, hoping she was wrong. Finally, her finger made contact.

"Hi, Jessica. Guess you've figured out by now that we left town." Deanne's voice was hushed. "Amy's doing fine, couldn't be happier, in fact. She's finally going to have a normal childhood, playing with a mommy who loves and can take care of her—"

Sam stopped the machine. "You don't need to listen to any more, Jessica. She's a sick woman."

Jessica made her way to Amy's room and collapsed on the bed, hugging the tiny baby pillow to her chest. She could hear Sam on the phone, calling in help. Before long, Becky arrived, along with Max and the cell phone he'd brought for her to use.

Max came to the bedroom door. "Jessica, I'll open this after we've listened to the message. We don't want to put you through that again."

She nodded as he closed it, frightened about what else Deanne may have said.

After a while, Sam came in to check on her, then, presuming she was asleep, he returned to the living room. Jessica hadn't answered, simply tired of claiming she was fine. She was far from it. She hurt physically and emotionally. Both went without saying, in her book anyway. She was angry, and she couldn't do anything to help. She hadn't meant to deceive him. She listened as Sam and Max set up call forwarding and Becky arranged for a phone tap.

"It's very unusual for the kidnapper to call the parents unless they're asking for ransom," Becky said quietly.

"Maybe she plans to," Sam suggested.

"Maybe she's tormenting Jessica." It was easy for Jessica to tell his dad's deep voice. "After she's frightened Jessica, could be that she's going to ask for money. Is Deanne that broke?"

"Not according to her bank account, but Sam found information leading us to believe she wants to adopt or go through a sperm bank to have a child on her own. She doesn't have nearly enough money to cover either, according to the pamphlets."

They obviously didn't realize Jessica could hear every word they said. She tried to tune them out, but she couldn't bear to miss anything they were saying about her daughter, no matter how much it frightened her.

"Haven't we had any more response from the Amber Alert?" Sam said, desperation in his voice.

"Nothing that's panned out. We've had local officers check every lead," Becky said. "Whatever we do, I want to be sure Amy isn't hurt, even if that means taking a little longer to apprehend Jones."

Jessica liked Becky and trusted her. She may not want children, but she had a true heart for them.

"I wish this was only about money. There's a sense of security in that."

"If it comes to that, you know we'll have no problem coming up with any amount she asks for," Max added. "If you need anything else, you know how to reach me."

Jessica heard the outside door close and assumed Max had gone home.

"If you have any leads you need—" Sam paused "—help with, Travis has offered his expertise."

Becky laughed. "You mean your brother's waiting for an invitation?"

Sam's laugh wasn't quite as jovial. "I asked him to stay out of it for now. I don't want anything spooking Deanne."

"Thanks, Sam. I know it's not easy to step back, but I think you're doing the right thing. I'm going to take the answering machine in and see if the techs can trace the number or come up with any additional clues from background sounds."

"Can you have someone bring another machine

over? I don't want to miss anything, just in case our call forwarding doesn't work out as planned.''

Jessica closed her eyes and hugged the pillow closer at Becky's cynical guffaw. ''Right, with one of your dad's phones?''

There was an odd silence, as if Becky had stopped midsentence. Even stranger, Sam didn't say a word in response. Jessica heard the door close and presumed she and Sam were again alone.

''Jessica,'' Sam said, right behind her. She jumped at the sound of his voice so close. She'd been straining to hear him whispering in the next room.

''Sorry, I didn't mean to startle you,'' Sam said in a quieter voice. ''We should probably look for anything out of place or missing before Becky leaves. I hate to disturb your rest…''

''You didn't disturb any rest, trust me.'' She swung her feet to the ground and sat up, then switched the bedside lamp on and looked around, blinking away the tears. ''Amy's bear is gone. At least she has that.''

''Maybe more light would help.'' Sam turned on the overhead light and offered her a hand. ''I looked in the drawers, but didn't notice much missing from the other night. You'd be a better judge of that.''

Jessica pressed her hands on her knees for support and walked over to examine the drawers as Sam knelt down and opened each one. ''I don't notice anything obvious, but it's hard to tell for sure.'' She checked through Amy's favorite outfits and none were missing. ''I suppose Deanne didn't want it to look obvious that she wasn't coming back. She probably bought her a few new outfits. That way we couldn't identify any of them.''

''You've obviously been thinking about this.''

She looked at Sam. "What else is there to think about right now?"

Sam looked hurt. "Guess I don't blame you. I can hardly get my mind off Amy, and I'm not even related."

"Yet," Jessica said softly, hoping to soothe his ego. "But you're as emotionally attached as if you were, I suspect."

His full lips formed a slight smile. "Why don't we look for that money you mentioned?"

"It's in my closet." She stepped around Sam and led the way. "I kept it in the blue-and-white shoe box on the top shelf, bottom of the stack. Could you reach it for me?"

Sam reached up, then paused. "It's on the top of the stack. Just a minute." He went into the other room and asked Becky for a pair of gloves so they could dust the box for fingerprints. "Was there any other reason for Deanne to have been in this closet, other than to get the money?"

"No, she never mentioned anything, and neither did I."

Sam pulled the box down and opened it. "Are these the right shoes?"

"Yes. You want to look for the money, or should I?"

"Go ahead," Becky answered. "Your prints would be on them anyway. We don't want to add Sam's to the mixture."

Jessica reached inside and found nothing in either shoe. "Looks like she's been playing me for a fool for a lot longer than I thought."

"You've only known her for approximately two months, right?"

Jessica nodded. "I must have mentioned the money about a month ago, at the Life Skills Class."

"Do you remember who all was in the class that day?"

She shook her head. "No, but Susan keeps a log of the attendees."

"Do you know about how much you had in there?"

"A thousand dollars. I kept meaning to deposit it in my account so it would be there for the earnest money on a house for Amy and me."

"When was the last time you looked to be sure the money was there?" Becky asked.

Jessica didn't need to think about that. "I added another hundred to it on payday last week."

"I'm curious," Becky said. "Why did you have a hidden stash instead of a savings account?"

"I started it a few years ago with however much I could sneak away from what Tim gave me for grocery money." She hated revealing so much about her marriage, but after Deanne's allegations, Jessica knew the police would have to know everything eventually. "When he died, I added a few hundred."

Sam's jaw tensed considerably. "Why did you keep it after Tim died?"

Jessica gave a moment's thought to his question and shrugged. "I didn't think much about it at first—it was a habit. Then when I moved in here, I knew I needed to move as soon as possible, so I kept adding to it when I could. I didn't have much choice of apartments after the accident. School was in session and I had to get out of military housing within thirty days. I didn't have an income of my own at the time. I was attending classes when the accident happened. I needed something cheap and close to medical care and the college. This wasn't easy with the stairs, but it was safe and within our budget. So I kept the stash for an emergency fund. I finished my sociology degree in December, and started working at the shelter full-time in June. I planned to keep adding to it every month—until I heard about this house coming available. Then I decided to use it for that.''

"Thanks. I'll add theft to the charges. I will need you to write all that you just told us in a statement for the case report,'' Becky added. "Did anyone else ever see that money?''

"My parents, when they came this summer.''

"Good. When you can, have Sam bring you to the station to give your statement.''

"Not a problem,'' Sam answered.

Becky left, and she and Sam were alone again. Jessica couldn't help but wonder if Sam had second thoughts. He'd alluded to Tim's abuse in his investigation of the accident, but she had never admitted it. "I'm sorry I didn't tell you about Tim's abuse then, Sam. I was afraid I'd lose Amy.''

"I suspected as much,'' he said quietly. He held out his hand. "It doesn't matter now. You're using your experience to try to help others avoid and overcome abusive relationships. I admire that.''

She took his hand and looked into his gentle, brown eyes. "Really? You don't think I'm a coward?''

"I've never thought you were a coward.''

There was an invitation in the smoldering depths of his eyes, and she was enthralled with his patience. He'd promised not to push her, and he'd kept that promise.

"We need to stay until an answering machine is delivered, right?''

Sam nodded.

"Why don't we have a soda? Are you hungry?"

"What are you offering?"

She opened the freezer. "One of your mother's casseroles."

"Oh, yeah," he said enthusiastically. He followed her to the kitchen and watched her put it into the microwave.

Jessica realized for the first time that Sam was wearing flannel sweatpants and a T-shirt, and looked quite comfortable. The T-shirt was old and thin and hugged his model physique.

"What else did Deanne say on the message?"

"Nothing you need to hear."

She stepped close and wrapped her hands behind his neck. "I know you want to protect me, Sam, but I'm really okay with hearing it all. You promised."

"I'm telling the truth—it's nothing that would help you right now. I told you there would be times I couldn't tell you everything. This is one of those times." Anger flashed in his eyes and Sam gently pulled her into his arms. "I can't stand to see you hurting anymore."

Jessica closed her eyes and rested her head on his chest. "What would I do without you?"

"Let's not find out," Sam said, and Jessica's lips sought his, calming her doubts and fears.

Chapter Sixteen

Two days had gone by without any news on Amy's disappearance. Sam and Lidia had done their best to keep Jessica busy, but despite their efforts, she was going stir-crazy. She hadn't been home since receiving Deanne's message, and at this point, no news wasn't necessarily good news. Especially from her perspective.

After eating Lidia's chicken cacciatore and angel hair pasta as a four-in-the-morning snack at her apartment, she and Sam had packed a few things in Jessica's suitcase.

The next day, Sam had gone to the precinct to catch up on work while Jessica and Lidia baked cookies and made cherry pies for a women's luncheon. Jessica had given out long before his mother, sleeping soundly from two until six. That evening while they watched a Western movie set in the Australian Outback, Sam asked her to go to church with him the next day.

Though she'd tried politely to get out of it, she'd finally agreed to go. Thoughts of her decision had interrupted her sleep all night. In one dream Jessica found herself saying the wrong thing to the pastor. In another she was singing off-key. When in a dream she was asked to read a passage from the Bible and couldn't find the right chapter, Jessica gave up on sleep. She knew God had turned a deaf ear to her requests.

On Sunday morning Jessica brushed her hair out and finished applying makeup with shaking hands. She hadn't been to church since seventh grade, when she had been asked to read the Scripture aloud and left the congregation in tears laughing, she'd been so nervous.

"I agreed with the mission statement of the shelter. I've given up drinking and parties. I'm being the best mother I can be," Jessica muttered. "No one said that attending church was a requirement of the job. Why can't You listen to me here at home, where I can't make a fool of myself? And if You're listening, please bring Amy home to me."

She slipped her feet into her shoes and opened the door, not expecting to be greeted by Sam's fist as he reached up to knock.

"That was close," he said with a smile. "You ready?"

Jessica touched his arm and felt his muscle tense. "I'm really tired. I didn't sleep very well last night, and I think one of us should stay home in case Deanne calls. Don't you?"

"You don't need to be nervous," Sam said with that truth-seeking radar of his. "There's nothing to be afraid of. I promise, no one will make you get up and say anything."

There he went reading her mind again. Jessica stepped back.

"What makes you say that?"

One shoulder lifted. "Our previous pastor asked visitors to introduce themselves. Gabriel doesn't usually. And if it'll make you feel better, I'll ask him specifically not to."

"You'll be up front, singing, right?" Now she was sounding paranoid.

"Jessica, there's really nothing to worry about. This isn't a test. It's a time to praise and worship God. There are weeks when it's the only peaceful time I have." He picked up a large folder and his Bible. "Let yourself relax and soak in His word. God knows what's on your heart today. For one hour, let yourself take your mind off Amy. And for the record, I play the keyboard, an electronic piano."

"Oh yeah, that's right," she said. *That's good, too,* she thought. *The pianist sits up front with the choir. Then I can hide in the back.* "And your parents don't go to this service?"

"They prefer the traditional service, so no, they usually don't go to this one. Are you okay?" Sam took her hand and Jessica nodded. "Hand the search over to God, honey. He can handle it a lot better than we can." He'd obviously read her mind again. "Just try to let God handle it for today."

Jessica couldn't imagine letting go of her worry and concern, even for an hour, but her going meant a lot to Sam. How could she not, after all he'd done for her this week?

"Can I get anything else for you? Did you take your pain medicine, antibiotics, anything else?"

"I'm okay, now, but if anyone mentions Amy…" Her eyes watered again and she added a few extra tissues to her purse as they walked out the door. "I'll manage. Where are your folks?"

"They have a group of friends they have breakfast

with on Sunday mornings after church, then Mom comes home and fixes Sunday dinner.''

"Why don't I spend the afternoon at my apartment? I hate to keep intruding on your family.''

"You're not intruding. Especially today. Lucia is working and Travis doesn't usually come on Sundays. Every now and then my brother's ex-wife, Emily, joins us, but that's usually it.''

"I know this is none of my business, but if your brother divorced Emily, isn't it extremely awkward that she's still so close to the family?''

"It's complicated.'' Sam led Jessica through the yellow-and-blue living room and entered the code to reset the security system. "There weren't many opportunities for a pediatric hematologist where Peter's work took him.''

"Where was that?'' Jessica asked as she found her purse.

"I can't remember where he was at the time. Like Dad, he traveled a lot.''

She looked at Sam suspiciously. "Is this another of those gray areas you can't tell me about?''

He laughed. "It really is a little unnerving how we seem to read each other's minds, isn't it?''

"Very. You don't happen to talk in your sleep, do you?'' She raised an eyebrow, unable to resist a momentary reprieve from the stress. "Listening at your door seems to be the only hope I have to learn any of your secrets.''

"I don't know, but maybe someday you'd like to find out for yourself.''

"Yeah, right, in my dreams,'' Jessica said with an overdose of sarcasm. They'd technically known each other a little more than a week, if they didn't consider her accident. Sam was far too logical to let their initial attraction get out of hand.

The drive to the church went quickly, and Jessica looked up at the bell tower and smiled. "This has to be one of the most beautiful churches in town. It reminds me of something out of *Arizona Highways*."

"I like the memorial gardens," he added as they walked through the formal entry to the church. "The church is rich with history. General Palmer was one of the original members."

"General Palmer, the man on the horse?"

"Yeah. Of course, the original church was a lot smaller."

Jessica paused to look at the stained glass. Jesus stood in the middle of a crowd with his arms open wide, as if welcoming a stranger.

Sam's voice interrupted her thoughts. "If you'd like, you could wait out here while I meet with the Praise Team in the sanctuary."

She turned quickly; she hadn't been aware that she was keeping him. "Can't I go ahead into the church and get a seat?" The gardens were beautiful, but she'd feel like a fish in a fishbowl out here as others were streaming inside. This was one week she didn't want to draw any attention to herself.

"Sure, we'll be warming up." He held out his hand, and Jessica accepted.

"So I could get a personal concert, huh?" She tipped her head slightly, wondering if Sam minded her teasing him.

Sam chuckled. "I hope we don't disappoint. I'd hate to have you leave before the rest of the choir arrives."

"I thought you said you're not part of the choir."

"Not a formal choir—the congregation. Those of us

at the front are just the music leaders to help everyone stay in sync. But without everyone singing, we're just a bunch of noisemakers.''

She wasn't sure whether he was teasing her or serious, but she figured she'd find out soon enough. Sam gave her hand a gentle squeeze as they walked into the sanctuary. "Have a seat anywhere. I'll see you in a bit.''

The sanctuary looked huge with its high ceiling. Along the side, the warm morning sunshine brought the stained-glass windows to their intended beauty. She gazed at a depiction of Jesus with children seated around him. Innocent children, before they'd made all of the mistakes she had. Children like Amy. Jesus welcomed them into his presence. How could such a loving God turn a deaf ear to a distraught and loving mother's plea to bring her daughter home?

Music filled the room with an upbeat tune, and Jessica, avoiding faces, found an empty pew and sat down. She watched Sam's every move. As one song blended into the next their eyes met and his smile soothed her rankled nerves. The seats began filling, and Jessica felt uncomfortable as a young couple sat next to her and welcomed her. She ventured a glance around the room, startled to see Susan Carter heading her way. Jessica turned away, and saw one of the volunteers from the shelter.

"Jessica," Susan whispered, "I'm so glad Sam convinced you to come with him.''

"I could hardly say no after he's done so much for me this week." Jessica looked around for Susan's twin daughters. "Where are Sarah and Hannah?''

Susan squeezed past Jessica and sat in the empty space between her and the young couple. "They went

to Sunday School and couldn't wait to help the teacher
clean up and get ready for Children's Church. How are
you doing?''

Jessica couldn't help but wonder if Susan had found
out Jessica was coming this morning and planned for
the twins to be busy just to ease Jessica's pain. ''About
as well as can be expected. I feel like I've had an arm
amputated. It's awful, Susan.'' Strange as it seemed,
Jessica hoped that if she kept Susan talking about the
kidnapping, she wouldn't notice that Jessica didn't
know any of the songs or customs of the service.

The last thing Jessica needed right now was to lose
her job over her faith, or lack thereof. Surely she could
play the part for an hour.

They visited quietly for a few minutes before the music faded and a young man opened the service. Then
everyone stood and began singing the words illuminated
on the screen to the right of the pulpit. Jessica soon
discovered that Susan was even more vivacious here
than at work. She raised her hands and swayed in
rhythm to the music, her beautiful voice carrying the
tune.

Certain that everyone must be staring, Jessica glanced
around, comforted to find Susan wasn't drawing any
attention in their direction. Sam's eyes were closed as
he sang to the music. The man on the guitar paused
between songs and prayed aloud. It wasn't a generic
''one prayer fits all'' kind of prayer she'd heard during
her childhood, but a contemporary worship of the Heavenly Father as the author of our lives. Jessica listened
with intense curiosity. The music served as a comforting
backdrop to the prayer, as if carefully choreographed.
Jessica felt the tension lift from her heart.

After another song, a teenager recited the Bible reading, and then a tall African-American man stepped to the front, welcoming members and visitors to Good Shepherd Christian Church. He invited everyone to greet their sisters and brothers in Christ, then stepped past the pulpit to mingle with the congregation. The Praise Team left the stage and moved to various seats in the congregation. Jessica saw Sam walk toward her, and her discomfort increased.

"How's it going?" he whispered as he squeezed into the pew beside Jessica.

Jessica simply nodded as the pastor motioned to be seated.

"Is this the pastor you've been talking so much about, Susan?" Jessica could see now why the new pastor had garnered her boss's attention.

Susan lifted her eyebrows and shrugged innocently.

"Our lives are continually filled with sin and sadness, yet generation after generation, history repeats itself. In times of turmoil like these, we as a community of God's children must come together to offer support and encouragement to those in need..."

Jessica glanced at Sam, not totally surprised by his wink. He discreetly offered his hand, and Jessica welcomed the warmth and comfort it gave her.

Reverend Dawson expounded on today's theme of God as the author of our lives, relating it to interactive games and movies, where the viewer can "choose" the ending. In the same way, he explained, we all make good and bad choices. God has planned each event in our lives so that we may see God and know Him and learn to rely on Him. "Through good times, do we remember to give God the credit?" Reverend Dawson asked. "Yet when tragedy strikes, we run to Him, lean on Him, and trust Him to fix our problems." Jessica knew she had been guilty of this. "Don't hide your head in shame, we've all been guilty of this spiritual tragedy. We claim credit for the successes, and expect God to remove our trials and tribulations. When we invite God into our lives, it's for eternity. Not just for here and now, or even yesterday and tomorrow. Eternity. Forever and always. He knows every minute of your life, the exact count of every hair on your head, every triumph and struggle."

Gabriel strolled to the pulpit and lifted his Bible. "In this book you can find endless examples of man's recurring fall from grace, and God's ultimate gift of His son, who died so that we may spend eternity in His presence." Gabriel read Scriptures, ending with Deuteronomy 30:19: "Moses said, 'I have set before you life and death, blessings and curses. Now choose life, so that you and your children may live.'"

During the closing prayer, Sam returned to his keyboard, and the music warmed her heart. She was so filled with God's overwhelming love that she didn't hear Gabriel's lead into Amy's kidnapping. He asked for her safe return, proclaiming that tragedy would not have the last word. "God's hope is eternal."

Jessica wiped away the tears as the reverend moved to the communion table and spoke about Christ's last supper with His disciples. Jessica was surprised to learn that even Thomas, one of Jesus's disciples, had doubted Jesus's identity, wanting to see the evidence of His resurrection for himself. When they were invited to share in the sacraments, Jessica accepted the bread and grape juice and invited God to be her Lord and Savior.

She left the church with encouragement and hope that God had not abandoned her, that all was just as He had planned. Now for the hard part: to go out into the world and keep this wonderful feeling twenty-four hours a day.

Chapter Seventeen

Sam helped Jessica out of the truck and into Galilee Women's Shelter. "You're doing really well this soon after your surgery."

"Thanks for the encouragement. Wish I were as convinced." Why couldn't he let her go home so she could let loose and cry? She greatly appreciated the Vance family's hospitality. Still, she wanted to convince them that she didn't require supervision.

Jessica's eyes misted over, but she refused to let anyone at work see her break down. She really didn't want to visit today, but they had no choice. Sam wanted her input on whether anything seemed out of place.

Susan met Jessica at the door and reached out to give her a hug. "Hi, Jessica. Morning, Sam. How are you two today?" Susan said cheerfully.

"Okay" was the best Jessica could come up with this morning. For a moment she caught herself resenting Susan's chipper mood.

"Morning, Jessica." The words echoed around them.

The receptionist offered her prayers and sympathy for what had happened.

Jessica hadn't slept a wink all night, and the hope from yesterday had faded. She couldn't fathom how anyone felt God could help in this. If He could, why hadn't He brought Amy home already, or kept it from happening in the first place? Despite her doubts, she thanked them. One mother had been reading her daughter a book and when she saw Jessica, she stood to leave.

"Hurry along, Tina, we don't want to bother these busy folks." Mandy made a wide turn to avoid Jessica.

"Susan, would you mind if we asked you some questions?" Sam watched the other residents, wondering if they were also going to treat Jessica as if she had a virus. Could any one of them have known Deanne had this planned?

Susan directed them into her office. "I think we'd be more comfortable talking here."

Sam watched as most of the residents offered Jessica their sympathy through a hug or even a simple smile. He realized Susan didn't seem to like the audience.

"You two go ahead," Jessica suggested. "I'll join you later."

Sam followed Susan, glancing back to see Jessica visiting with a few of the residents. He was startled by the dreariness of the facilities, though the lobby had been brightened considerably with new paint and a colorful quilt.

Susan closed the door, which made Sam wonder what could be so private. "So, does this mean you've come up with something?"

"I wish it did." Susan rounded the desk and sat down. "I just felt it would be wise to avoid upsetting the residents any more than they have been. We've had a couple of families leave, thinking they're going to be safer on the streets.''

"That's frightening. What's scared them away? Could they have helped Deanne set this up?''

Susan shook her head. "No, they're too upset to have been involved. I could never really put my finger on what bothered me about Deanne. I suspect it's similar for the others.''

Sam looked at her, startled. "What do you mean?''

Susan shrugged, uncomfortable with something. Surely it couldn't have been too bad; or she wouldn't have left her twin daughters in Deanne's care.

"It was my first instinct. I thought I was uncomfortable with her scars. She did fine with the kids and took great care of them. There was just something off about her.''

Jessica knocked and came in and sat down without a word.

Sam met her dazed expression. "Anything?'' Jessica simply shook her head and Sam turned back to Susan.

"Did you know she had a daughter?'' Sam asked.

Susan leaned forward, her eyes wide. "She what? Deanne never mentioned a daughter to me.'' She looked first at Jessica, then at Sam. "Did you know anything about a daughter, Jessica?'' Jessica shook her head. "Oh, please don't tell me the child was removed from Deanne's custody.''

"No, nothing like that. She died in the same fire that injured Deanne.'' Sam barreled into the next questions, trying to avoid looking at Jessica, afraid that if she started crying, he wouldn't be able to continue. "What do you know about her injuries?''

"Only that she was injured in a fire a little over a year ago. She lived at the shelter for a few weeks after being released from the hospital. I believe she'd moved here from Kansas.'' Susan glanced at Jessica. ''When she made it into her own home, the previous director agreed to let her help at the center. She does a—''

''I'm going to go to my office and check my mail,'' said Jessica.

Sam took her hand as she tried to escape. ''Are you feeling okay?''

''Fine. I just need a break from all of this.''

She probably wanted a break from him, as well. They had been through these same questions over and over again.

Jessica closed the door behind her, and Sam heaved a sigh of relief. At least she was letting herself react to her emotions.

''How's she really doing, Sam?''

He knew Susan from church, and he trusted her. ''I'm worried about her. I assume you know Jessica was also in an accident not so long ago. Now this. I'm not sure how she's hanging on, but she is putting on a brave face. I thought going to church yesterday really helped, but today, she seems lower than before.''

''I can't imagine the agony she's going through.''

He'd wanted to get another opinion, and supposed Susan knew as much as anyone could. ''How would you describe Jessica?''

She sent him a puzzled look. ''How do you mean?''

''I want someone who can show me another perspective on her. I need to try to figure out why Deanne would take Amy from Jessica. If I didn't know her at all, what would you tell me about her?''

Susan smiled. ''Jessica is a fun and caring woman. She's had a few rough breaks, but she's strong. Considering her back problems, she's still a wonderful mother. It's not an easy job on a good day, you know, but when a single mom doesn't feel well, there's no choice but to carry on.'' Susan interwove her long fingers and leaned forward on the desk.

"I see. Does she miss much work?"

"This week is her first time off since she started two months ago. She takes her lunch hour for doctors' appointments, refuses to use her sick time."

Sam thought about his mother's comment about Jessica's faith, but instead asked, "Any idea if there have been any disagreements between Jessica and Deanne?"

"Not that I'm aware of. But Jessica would go directly to Deanne if there was something wrong, that's her style."

He had to know. "Any idea where she is in her faith?"

She pursed her lips and shook her head. "She agreed with our mission statement, which indicates a belief in God, but nothing too overwhelming. To be honest, I don't think that means the same thing to everyone, and technically, it's illegal to ask for much more detail these days. You can imagine how happy I was to see her yesterday. It's the first I've seen her at our church."

Sam nodded. "I know."

Susan looked at him with laughter in her eyes. "Oh, have you been keeping your eye on her for long?"

"No, but she's the type of woman who's hard to miss. I've seen her at the Stagecoach Café a lot lately."

Susan nodded. "Oh yes, with the bachelors... Um, you didn't think she was dating all of them, did you?"

"The thought did go through my mind, for a while, but that part is cleared up."

"I'd hope so. It seems like you two have hit it off."

"Yeah, I wish she were as convinced of that. Time

will tell, I guess. It's not been an easy week to think of—'' His voice cut out, as if he was sixteen again. He cleared his throat, willing his brain to catch up with the conversation.

''Romance?''

He shook his head, embarrassed that his brain had stalled on that particular word.

Susan laughed. ''God created *amour* too, you know. Read Song of Solomon sometime.''

''That stall wasn't intentional. For the record, I have no aversion to romance.''

''That's comforting to know, since the news is that you're courting my dear friend.'' Susan's onyx-colored eyes sparkled with laughter.

Sam shrugged. ''Let's see, have you been talking to my mother, or Lucia? Because Jessica certainly wouldn't have admitted as much.''

''All in God's time.''

''I have to admit, He's really caught me off guard this time. Having one of us a little gun-shy makes for a good balance, since the timing is less than wonderful.''

''Our hearts just never seem to work logically, do they.''

Sam agreed, then changed the subject, relieved to not be talking about falling in love. They discussed Deanne again, and Susan looked for records from her interview but couldn't find them.

''I don't understand,'' Susan said, riffling through files. She opened the next drawer, and the next, and looked through them all. ''I can't imagine when she could have come in and gotten her file out of here.''

''Maybe someone got it out for Detective Hilliard earlier in the investigation. I'll check on that.''

Susan stared at him as if in a daze. "It's so unbelievable. I keep praying that Amy will come home unharmed. Oddly enough, I don't question Amy's safety with Deanne. But if there is someone else involved, you can never be certain."

Sam closed his eyes, unwilling to think of the terrible things that had happened in similar cases. "Do you know if there was anyone in Deanne's life?"

"No one that I'm aware of, but she worked more closely with the child-care staff than with me. They may know. I hate to pass the buck. Since I'm the director, I should have looked into the personnel files more thoroughly when I started."

"It may not have made any difference—her official record appears to be clean up until recently."

"How recently?" Susan sat up straighter. "What did she do?"

"Afraid I can't divulge that information at this point. And it may be nothing at all." Sam wished he hadn't brought his own suspicions into the discussion.

"I'm her employer, she worked with children. Shouldn't that matter?" Susan's curls bounced with each motion she made.

Sam did his best to calm Susan down. "It's just suspicion at this point. She hasn't been charged with anything. And we didn't know she worked with children until this incident. It's not like you'd let her come back at this point. Would you?"

Susan's jaw dropped. "Of course not! Unless... Never mind. If it was some sort of emergency, she'd have called by now. I just can't seem to accept that Deanne planned this out and actually took Amy." She shook her head. "How could anyone do such a thing?"

"The human psyche is a dangerous element to mess

with. When we don't take care of it, these things happen. Deanne should have sought psychiatric help." Sam looked around, realizing he was preaching to the choir. Susan and the other staff at Galilee Women's Shelter were obviously trying to help a hurting segment of the population. "Well then…" Sam stood up and stepped toward the door. "I'm sure someone will get back to you if we have any more questions."

"I'd like that file back, if they have it. Or at least a copy for our records." Susan stood with a hand on her hip.

Sam smiled at her determination to do things right. "If you'd like to consider reviewing the rest of your employee records, I'd be happy to assist you with some ideas about how you can go about it legally."

"We'll talk about that after we find Amy."

"Thanks," Sam said as he opened the door. "Which way to Jessica's office?"

"End of the hall, to the left."

Sam followed the hall and stepped into the last office, surprised to find Jessica nowhere in sight. He spun around and looked in each room along the way back to the lobby. Surely she wouldn't try to leave without him. Surely she knew the police were doing everything they could to find Amy. She couldn't do any more. He saw the receptionist and stopped.

"Do you know where Jessica went?"

"Next door, to the child-care room, I think." She gave him directions on how to get there, and Sam rushed outside and into the next entrance, following the noise to the children. *Please, Lord, don't let her run away from me. Don't let her take off trying to find Amy on her own. Take care of her and help me to show her how much she is loved.*

As he ran into the room, he saw Jessica standing at the exit to the outside play area.

"Jessica?"

She pushed herself away from the door frame, where she'd been watching the children play.

"Amy should be here, playing with her friends."

"You scared me," he growled. "I thought you said you'd be in your office." Sam ordered his heart to slow down.

She turned around, revealing red eyes. "I did what I needed to there, and came to see if I could find anything in here that might help us find them." Jessica folded her arms in front of her, challenging him to push.

Sam waited a minute, trying not to sound defensive. "You could have let me know." It didn't do any good. He and Jessica had been locking horns all morning. The only thing he'd done right in her eyes was bringing her here, with him.

"I'm not the one in trouble, Sam. Yet I seem to be the one with the bodyguard."

She walked past him, and Sam took a deep breath. "Patience, Sam," he whispered, reminding himself not to overreact. She'd been through a lot in the last week. He counted to ten, then turned to follow her out. She'd already hurried out the front door and was making her way through the wrought-iron-surrounded yard as if he were a threat to her safety.

"Jessica…" Sam nodded to the security guard as he walked past. "Have a good day."

"You, too, Detective."

Sam hurried his step to catch up, hoping to talk some sense into her. "Slow down or you're going to hurt yourself." She stepped through the iron gate and slammed it closed.

Sam tugged on it, but it had locked automatically. He looked up, the sharp pointed tips discouraging him from climbing over.

"Just a minute…" the security officer said as he rushed to the gate.

Wasn't that just like God to test his patience the minute he asked for an extra dose? Sam thought. She may have slowed him down, but she could still hear him. "You're supposed to be resting. Taking it easy. I shouldn't have let you come in the first place."

The security officer paused before opening the gate. "Can I do anything to help, Jessica?" he asked.

"I'm fine, Edgar. Give me a block and let him out."

Sam looked at the guard and shrugged. "She just had surgery a few days ago, I'm only trying to keep her from getting hurt." The guard opened the gate and Sam jogged to meet her.

"I don't need anyone to tell me how to take care of myself, or where I can or can't go," she insisted as she passed the pickup. "I feel like I'm in a prison surrounded by guards. And I haven't done anything wrong."

Sam stopped at the pickup and opened the passenger door, hoping she would listen. "Get back here and we'll talk about it," he said in an even tone. The one place he didn't want in any way to appear bossy was outside a shelter for abused women. "Jessica. There's no need to push yourself so hard."

She spun around too quickly and crumpled to her knees.

Sam hurried down the block. "I told…"

Jessica glared at him. "Don't even think of saying it, Sam. I only twisted my ankle." She gathered her skirt around her knees and slowly moved to get up.

"And landed on the ground." He knelt next to her, offering a hand. "Are you sure you're okay?"

"Positive."

"I'm not trying to be a thorn in your side, Jessica. I'm just trying to make sure you take care of yourself, since you don't seem to realize your limitations."

She batted his hand away and pushed herself to her feet.

"When's your checkup?" He couldn't believe she'd brush him aside and ignore her own health. Jessica stepped close enough to kiss, but he knew better.

"I don't know, and right now, I don't care. And I don't want you looking into it for me."

"Maybe someone needs to," he said in his "just-the-facts" voice. "I know this isn't easy, Jessica. You haven't had anyone around to take care of you in a long time. And I know this isn't the best time to start a relationship, but I can't just turn my back."

"And who is it that isn't seeing their own limitations? You can't make my back heal any faster. You can't keep me from getting hurt, emotionally or physically. Just like Reverend Dawson said in his sermon yesterday, you can't fulfill me. Only God can do that."

Sam stepped back, shocked to hear a lesson in faith coming from her mouth.

Chapter Eighteen

Sam had watched Jessica make her way to the communion table, thrilled for the revelation. Now, three days later, he still couldn't quite believe Jessica had had such a quick change of heart. He couldn't help but wonder if she'd sincerely given herself to God. Her life and emotions rose and fell like a roller coaster.

Sam went to work, hoping the time apart would be good for both of them. They needed time away from one another, and he needed to remind himself of the real world, which included finding a way to link Barclay to the Valenti murder. He'd stopped in to visit with an informant on the way to the office. As usual, Rodney didn't answer the door right away.

"You ought to know better by now, Rodney," Sam muttered. He knocked again, raising his voice this time. "I know you're not even awake yet, let alone out of the house." He waited. Finally, the door opened. "Morning," Sam said to the man with the dreadlocks and scruffy beard.

Rodney's eyes opened wide. "Oh man, I already told your partner that I didn't know the doctor."

"Which partner came to visit?" Sam had only told one person about his suspicions. If Rodney guessed incorrectly, Sam would know he was using again.

"You know, that tall dude. Sully, I think it was."

"Fine, I'll talk to him about Valenti. But I'm here to ask about someone else. You have a minute?"

The guy looked outside and motioned Sam into the kitchen. "This is a little early to stop in, Detective. You haven't been around much lately. What's going on?"

Sam took a sip of his take-out coffee and sat down across the table from Rodney. "I've had some personal issues to deal with." He pulled Deanne's picture from his pocket. "You seen her before?"

"Once or twice." He looked at Sam from under his blond dreads.

Sam exhaled loudly, noting the tidy but definitely low-budget accommodations Rodney was setting up. Looked like he was staying clean, despite working around a highly disreputable crowd at the Longhorn Saloon. It probably hadn't changed considerably from the cowboy bar of the early pioneer days.

"What does she do?"

Rodney rubbed his shoulder. "I seen her in the kitchen now and then, talking with Campy. She buys an ounce or so of heroin every other month or so, something about the doctors and red tape. She needs pain medicine. Those are some nasty scars she has. Cut her some slack."

"Do you happen to know if she's seeing anyone in particular?"

"Naw, she's pretty much a loner, with those scars and all."

Sam had to admire the fact that Jessica hadn't let the same prejudices stop her from trusting Deanne. But for an instant, he selfishly wished she *had* been just a little less trusting. They wouldn't be searching for Amy if Jessica trusted her instincts. "I noticed that she moved here from out of state. Any chance she's done any transporting?"

Sam was playing a long shot, but if she had out-of-state connections, he wanted to know just who they were dealing with.

Rodney looked at her picture again. "She may look rough now, but no, I don't think she has what it takes to be a mule."

Sam stood up and headed toward the door. "Find out for me. You know my number."

He spent the day working on his cases with Sully, then headed toward his parents' house, anxious to see Jessica.

"I thought you might like to get out," he said when he saw her. "I need to pick up a few clean clothes and get my keyboard so I can start practicing for Adam and Kate's wedding, not to mention the praise music for church next week. We could go out to eat or fix dinner at my place."

"Sounds interesting. When do you practice with your team?"

Sam wanted to smile but didn't. It was becoming very clear that Jessica hadn't spent much time in contemporary churches. "Praise Team meet every Wednesday."

She frowned. "What if we're not here Wednesday?"

She sounded so certain that they'd be gone, he wondered if she'd heard something that he hadn't. "If I'm not here, they'll continue without the keyboard. Is there a change with the search?''

Her smile disappeared and she shook her head in silence. ''What about the wedding? Do they have a backup in case you can't make it?''

Sam sensed Jessica felt some change was near and he didn't want to discourage her. ''We're all going to make it. I want you and Amy to come with me. And I'm sure Adam and Kate would love to have you there. Right now we all need to see the good guys win.'' Sam struggled to keep his distance after her comment earlier in the week. It never would have occurred to him that she thought he was trying to replace God in her life, especially a woman that he was beginning to consider spending the rest of his life with. Jessica Mathers continuously caught him by surprise. Though she denied needing him, he knew better. He felt the way she hugged him, that ''don't ever let go'' intensity. And he was beginning to realize just how much that meant to him as well.

''Sam?'' Jessica stepped closer. ''What's wrong?''

''Wrong?'' What made her think something was wrong?

''You mentioned the wedding, and now you're staring at me as if something's wrong.''

He shook his head. ''Nothing's wrong.''

''Then why are you clear over there?''

He looked at the distance between them and shrugged. ''I thought you wanted some space.''

She blushed. ''Sorry. I've been a little off-kilter this week. I know I've been confusing.''

''To borrow one of your favorite phrases, 'now that's an understatement.' You feeling any better?''

She nodded. ''A little, all things considered. What

I'm trying to say is yes, I'd like to run errands with you tonight. But I don't want to go out to eat, if you honestly don't mind.'' She hesitated. ''I can't take any more sympathy right now. I know everyone means well, but...''

''You don't have to explain to me. I'd just as soon have the time alone with you.''

''Let me get a few things.''

''You won't need anything.''

She looked at him oddly. ''I...*need* to take my purse, at least. And the cell phone.''

''Okay. I'm going to tell Mom and Dad where we're going. Get whatever you need.''

While they were driving across town, Jessica's parents called to see if they'd heard anything, bringing tears to Jessica's eyes. ''No, Mom, you wouldn't be able to do anything if you were here. Trust me, Sam and his family are taking very good care of me, and Sam's a detective.'' He saw a smile lift the corners of her full lips. ''Yeah, same one.''

Sam wondered if she'd figured out that his father also had law enforcement connections. If she did, she didn't mention it. He had spent a lot of time lately thinking about her family. She didn't seem very close to them, but then, she mentioned that they had spent a long period of time here after her accident and again this past summer. Were they still working through childhood rebellion issues, or were they past that now?

Sam pulled to a stop to enter the code to the gated community where his house was located. He saw Jessica's mouth drop open, and she quickly finished her conversation and clicked the phone off.

''Mom and Dad want to come,'' she told Sam. ''I

told them there's nothing they can do, but that doesn't matter to them."

He noticed she hadn't mentioned they were becoming personally involved. "Have you told them we're sort of…well, not really, but…"

"Dating? No, I—" She looked at his modest house and smiled. "This house looks just like your type."

Laughing, he pulled into his driveway, opening the garage door with a push of the button. He didn't want anyone noticing that he was home. He wanted them to have some peace and quiet. "Is that a compliment?"

"Of course it is," she said with a laugh. "I really like this southwestern adobe style. It reminds me of Italy."

Sam closed the door and they were encased in darkness. "So what did you tell your parents? Hopefully you know I wouldn't insult you by considering this actual dating. One day, I'll do it properly."

"They asked if you're the same Sam that was on my case after the accident. I said yes. I didn't know quite how to explain what's happening between us. One disastrous date usually doesn't lead to the kind of relationship we have."

"Which is?"

Jessica shrugged. "My brain tells me not to commit to anything right now, but sometimes I think it's a little late. My heart never has been very patient, and last time, it was a huge mistake."

Sam pressed his lips to hers. "I'd like to say I'm a patient man, but I promised I'd never lie to you. Then again, I certainly don't want to be considered another mistake. I hope you'll realize how much I care about your physical, spiritual and emotional well-being, Jessica. I know there's a lot on your mind right now. Just

knowing I'm also on your mind is enough for now."
He helped her out of the truck and led her into the
house. "Make yourself comfortable."

Jessica looked around and smiled. "This is really
nice, Sam. Did you decorate, or did your mom?"

"I had a little help, but I did a lot of it myself." He
opened the refrigerator and set a bag of groceries inside.
"Pork chops or steak?"

"You went shopping?" Jessica stepped into the rus-
tic-looking kitchen and leaned against the counter. She
ran her hand across the marble countertop in silence.

"No. Mom went shopping and I begged a few groceries off of her. She was happy to contribute to the
cause." Sam tried to contain his smile, but when she
burst out laughing, he gave up.

"I'm sure she's leaps and bounds ahead of us in planning."

"She's not terribly subtle, is she."

Jessica blushed again. "No, but she means well. I
guess what surprises me is Max. He seems so gruff at
times, and at others, he's all heart. He told me that when
he met your mom it was love at first sight."

"That's encouraging, isn't it?" Sam hadn't considered that he and his father were much alike, but as he
thought about it now, Sam realized that the older he
got, the more he understood his dad. Sometimes, as in
this issue with Barclay, he wished he didn't understand
quite so well.

"Encouraging? How do you mean?"

Sam led her outside to the backyard, which over-
looked the Garden of the Gods and Colorado Springs.
"Trusting your heart. That sometimes, we have to listen
to our instincts."

"That's easier said than done," she said, wandering

to the rock waterfall. She stared at it, holding herself tight. "I think I'm on the right track, and then reality hits again."

"Such as?" Sam liked seeing her here, and wondered how she'd feel about living in a modest detective's home on Goldmine Lane overlooking the beautiful front range of Colorado.

"You'd laugh," she said, glancing at him over her shoulder.

"I won't laugh." He stepped behind her and wrapped his arms around her. "What is your instinct telling you?"

"I was reading a book your mother gave me today and I felt this incredible peace. Like God had taken the worry of Amy's disappearance off my shoulders. I saw Deanne."

"You saw her?"

"Probably my imagination conjuring things up while I was napping. She was driving back here."

Sam closed his eyes, willing himself to keep quiet. She didn't need a dose of reality right now. "I hope you're right."

Jessica turned her head to meet his and kissed his cheek. "Thank you for taking me to church, Sam. It was so different from when I was young. It's almost like I don't need to worry anymore, that God will bring her home."

"Miracles do happen, Jessica, but I don't think we should stop looking yet."

"I know. All week long I've been finding so many signs of comfort. One verse said, 'When you pass through deep waters, I will be with you; your troubles will not overwhelm you.' Am I grasping at straws, Sam, or doesn't that mean that God is here, lifting my burdens?''

Sam felt at odds with her question. He wanted to encourage her to trust God but worried that she would ignore reality. "Yes, it does, but…"

She took a step and turned to face him. "But what?"

"We can't use God as a crutch, Jessica." How could he relate his feelings to her? "For example, we all sin, there's no doubt about that, but what I mean is…" He took a deep breath and let it out. "We shouldn't deliberately sin, knowing that God will forgive us."

She looked confused. "Not worrying is sin?"

"No, that was just an example. I'm glad you're feeling better, but it may be that your hormones are leveling out, or the anesthesia is having less effect on your system, or—"

She laughed. "So you think it was simply a chemical reaction that made me overreact, and God had nothing to do with easing my tension?"

"I didn't mean that at all. You have every right to be upset, and you're dealing with it very well." Sam felt as if he was getting himself into deep water and prayed that God would help clear the air between him and Jessica. "I hope you're right, that Deanne's on her way back here, but from my professional experience, I'd say it's not likely that she'd come back here." Sam watched the evening breeze blow her hair off her shoulders. "I have all the faith in eternity, and believe beyond any shadow of a doubt that God is taking care of Amy. But I'm not going to sit and wait for them to get here. If we get a lead, I'm going to do everything within my power to find them. That doesn't mean I don't believe God isn't there with me every step of the way."

She looked at him with moist eyes. "I guess that's

why God gave you to me right now, to keep me from being confused and messing everything up.''

''And why'd He give you to me, then?''

She pressed her lips to his, then pulled away. ''He's testing your patience.''

''That He is.'' Sam kissed her again, more deeply, then led her into the house to fix dinner.

Jessica opened the bag of salad greens and rinsed them, then cleaned the potatoes and put them into the microwave. Throughout the evening, Sam worried that Jessica had misunderstood his comments about accepting Christ into her life.

After dinner and dishes Jessica rested on the sofa while Sam organized the music and played through each song. His mind drifted back to Jessica's questions about him not being around for practice or church this week. He watched her sleeping peacefully, a rare occurrence since her surgery, despite the medicine that was supposed to make her sleepy. He hated to wake her, but it was nearly midnight and he needed to get some sleep, too.

His cell phone rang, making them both jump. He answered and listened anxiously.

By the time Becky finished giving him details, Jessica was fully alert. ''Was that Becky?''

He nodded. ''They've found Deanne's car.''

Chapter Nineteen

"And Amy?" Jessica said in barely a whisper. "Did they find her?"

Sam shook his head. "Not yet, but this is a start. They want you to identify some of Amy's belongings."

Her heart stopped. "She's not—"

"No." Sam took hold of her arms and pulled her close. "No, there's no sign of them. Right now, they think Deanne abandoned the car. Either it wasn't working, or she heard the Amber Alert and thought she was less likely to be recognized without her car. They didn't take much with them, apparently. And her car wasn't in good shape to start with."

Jessica felt the dizziness envelop her and she took a deep breath. "Where is it?"

"Pagosa Springs, in southwestern Colorado. I'm going to call Dad, see if he can book a flight as soon as possible. That's probably going to be tomorrow morning. Becky will be going, too. I'll pack a few things and then we'll go get your bag ready."

She didn't tell him that she didn't usually fly on small

aircraft. Claustrophobia was nothing to be embarrassed about, but all things considered, she had to put her own fears aside for Amy's sake.

From the sound of her tossing and turning, Jessica hadn't slept all night. He'd learned to sleep with his door open so he could listen for her. She in turn had found his father's oil can and fixed the squeaking door, forcing himself to sleep lighter in order to keep watch on her.

At dawn, they drove to the airport with Becky and caught a flight to Durango. As soon as they boarded the plane, Sam noticed Jessica's shoulders tense and he watched her take long deep breaths. Despite her efforts, soon she was almost panting.

"Are you okay?"

She didn't look at him, just kept her nose to the window and nodded quickly. She refused to buckle her seat belt until the last minute, and didn't make a move to converse with him or Becky from takeoff to landing forty-five minutes later. It wasn't until she was again outside that he realized the problem. She was claustrophobic, and the puddle-jumper flight they'd taken only held about a dozen passengers, so it wasn't too roomy.

"You should have said something, Jessica."

"I did what needed to be done. I'm fine now," she said.

The sheriff met them at the airport and took them directly to Deanne's car, which had been impounded in the city lot.

"Could you show us where you actually found the car?" asked Sam.

"Sure. Take a look at the car, then we'll head up the mountain." He mentioned that the doors were locked when they found it. "It looks like she was headed west on Highway 160 over Wolf Creek Pass." He handed Becky a stack of photographs of the outside and inside of the car and skid marks. "We can have a mechanic look at it and see if she had car trouble. She and a child caught a ride into town with a delivery truck. He dropped them off at the first service station, but the trucker became suspicious when the woman never went inside to make arrangements. We have an officer checking nearby hotels and buses to see if she's been there."

Sam knelt down and felt under the car for a spare key holder. "Do you know where we can reach the driver who brought her into town?"

"That info is in here. He heard the Amber Alert about an hour down the road and called me." The sheriff gave Becky a copy of the file. "I've contacted a rental company to send a car over for you."

"Thanks," Sam said, coming up dry in his search for the key.

Jessica confirmed that the clothing and blanket were Amy's. When the rental car arrived, they followed the sheriff to the location. After a long day of investigating, they found out Deanne and Amy had stayed at the hotel near the hot springs for two nights, then caught a bus to Flagstaff, Arizona. Sam called Jake to see if he had anything, and to let him know that it had become a federal case. It was time they officially called in the FBI.

"Did you find anything helpful in her computer?" Sam asked his friend.

Jake answered with his usual arrogant humor. "Isn't that what you wanted me to do? Of course I found it. She has several e-mail letters from a friend in Phoenix, the last of which mentioned she's looking forward to meeting her and her daughter.''

Sam sighed with relief and his vision blurred.

"You there? Sam?"

"I'm just so relieved. After looking at the car, I had this sick feeling in the pit of my stomach. I have hope again. Thanks."

"Glad I could help. I'll call if I find anything else." Jake gave Sam the address and name of the friend.

"If you could, leave a message at my precinct number if you don't reach the cell phone. We've been in and out of service areas, and I don't want you to think I've gotten a message that I haven't."

"Will do. Take care, Sam."

Sam plugged his cell phone in to charge while he went across the hall to tell Becky and Jessica the news. He could see the excitement in their faces, too.

After Becky called the Phoenix PD, the three of them went to a steak house for dinner where a live country-western band raised the roof with knee-slapping music. Sam was so happy he even talked Jessica into trying their timing at a Texas two-step.

"We'll find her," Sam said, pulling her close while they waited for the next song to start.

"I know. I wish we could get there tonight. Do you really think Deanne is going to meet this person?" The music started and Jessica moved to the beat.

"I'm not really sure, but it's a step in the right direction. The Phoenix police will keep an eye out for Deanne at the bus stop, and there is a stakeout at the friend's house."

She didn't reply, and Sam decided to just enjoy their time together. He liked the way her hand fit into his and the synchronization they had as dance partners.

"Break?" she said at the end of the next song.

"I'm sorry, you should have said something earlier," he replied. She squeezed his hand as they returned to the empty table, where they found a note from Becky scribbled on the napkin. Sam read it with a smile. "Becky walked back to the hotel," he said. "You've been pretty quiet today. Are you feeling okay?"

"I didn't sleep very well last night. I was anxious for the trip today."

"You should have told me you were claustrophobic."

She shrugged. "It's okay. Neither of us had had enough rest to drive safely."

"No, you shouldn't be driving at all." He dropped his fist to the table suddenly. "You missed your checkup, didn't you? When was the last time anyone looked at your back?"

She shrugged, and Sam looked more closely at her. Her skin was flushed, and her usually bright eyes looked dull and tired. "We should get back to the hotel and get you to bed," he said as he leaned out of the wood booth to get the waitress's attention.

She smiled weakly. "Yeah, I'm beat."

Jessica and Becky were sharing a room at the motel, and Sam had ended up down the hall, thankful for even the tiny rooms that they'd been able to procure at the last minute. He lifted his hand to her forehead, recalling now that her hand had felt unusually warm when they'd danced. He hadn't thought too much about it, he realized, had just figured it had been a warm day at a high altitude and they'd spent much of it outdoors. "You feel feverish—maybe you should have Becky check your back and make sure it doesn't look infected."

The waitress dropped off the bill and Sam checked the figures.

"I just need some rest. I don't need Becky to check it." She seemed to melt into the support of her hands.

"Then I will."

She raised an eyebrow and gave him a slight smile. "Don't you wish."

He felt a deep longing inside at her teasing words. "You missed your doctor's appointment. Someone is going to check it. If it isn't me, and it isn't Becky..." He paused as he reached into his hip pocket for his wallet. "I guess we only have one other choice." He slipped a department-issued credit card into the slot and looked for the waitress.

Even over the twang of music, a loud crash of dishes and silverware made him drop the bill valet to the floor. He turned to find Jessica's head smack-dab in the middle of Becky's plate of leftover chicken-fried steak and mashed potatoes.

Sam lifted her face out of the plate and shook her gently. "Waitress!" He yelled as he checked Jessica's pulse and breathing. "Jessi!"

The waitress and manager rushed across the room to make sure no one was hurt. "Should we call an ambulance?"

"Yeah, would you? I'm not familiar with town, and I think we'd better get her checked out."

One waitress ran to the phone, and another took her place, offering a stack of napkins, then a clean, cold, wet dishcloth. Sam washed her face while the staff cleaned the table and took care of the bill. A few minutes later, Sam heard the warble of the ambulance sirens. The music stopped when the uniformed men rolled the gurney through the restaurant. While Sam held her steady, the EMT took her blood pressure. The female medic cleared the mattress and pulled a small ammonia inhalant capsule from a huge bag, popped it open and waved it under Jessica's nose, making her cough.

As he recited the blood pressure, the man reached for her other arm. "Let's lift her on three, and lay her on the gurney. Where are you from?"

"Colorado Springs. Jessica had back surgery a week ago. She's been under tremendous stress. Her daughter was kidnapped, and we're here following a lead on the case."

Both EMTs looked at him as if he'd lost his mind. "You gotta be kidding us."

"I wish I were. I'm a detective with the Colorado Springs Police Department." Sam showed his badge and then clipped it back to his belt.

After a quick discussion about whether to lay her on her back or side, Jessica woke up enough to voice her preference, and they were on the way to the hospital.

As Sam followed the ambulance, he called Becky with an explanation. "Why'd you leave the restaurant without telling us?" he asked.

"I thought Jessica was so quiet because she was uncomfortable around me," she said over the scratchy connection.

"Why would she be uncomfortable?" Sam was trying to keep up with the ambulance, thankful that he hadn't tried to find the hospital himself. The mountain town seemed to be full of narrow one-way roads that led to nowhere.

Becky gave her usual guffaw and Sam could imagine her eyes rolling. "I get the very strong feeling that she has figured out that we dated."

"Yeah, so?"

This time she laughed. "You aren't exactly the kind of man a woman wants to share, Sam. Especially with an ex-girlfriend."

Sam shook his head. "Thanks for the flattery, Becky, but I think it's more physiological than psychological. Hey, we're at the hospital. I'll call you with an update."

"Take care. I'll keep making phone calls. Nothing new yet."

He waited in the lobby while the staff got her into a gown to examine her, then they called him into the room.

"The doctor's on the phone with her surgeon. She'll be right with you," said a nurse.

They waited another hour, with Jessica dozing off and on. Due to the high altitude, they were also giving her oxygen. Her bangs were plastered back from the cleaning solution and he noticed butterfly bandages over a small cut on her forehead. The automated blood pressure monitor hissed itself full and slowly deflated every fifteen minutes.

Finally the doctor returned. "Good evening, Detective Vance. Sorry for the delay, her surgeon had an emergency." She smiled and leaned against the counter. "I'd like to put Jessica on IV antibiotics to fight the infection, and on fluids because she may be dehydrated. Did she drink much water while you were out in the sun today?"

"Some, but probably not enough. So what happened? Is it the infection, or the altitude, or what? Is she okay?"

"She'll be fine. As you said, she's had a stressful week. With the lack of sleep that you indicated, combined with the sudden elevation difference and an emotional day in strong sunshine, I suspect it's all of the above.''

''Did she have an emotional breakdown?''

The doctor looked surprised. ''Not from what you've told me. I'm sure that she's been emotional and distraught, but under the circumstances, those are very normal reactions. I believe this is physiologically induced.''

''How long does she need to stay here?'' he asked.

''The nurse will be in soon to start the IV, then I'd like to wait a couple of hours after it's through dripping to see if she's feeling better. Would you like something to drink?''

''Sounds like a glass of water wouldn't be a bad idea. Thanks.''

When she returned with the water she added, ''I understand she's going to want to leave the hospital as soon as possible. I prescribed medicine that will help her moods and help her sleep a little more. I did discuss it with her doctor. We feel her current medication isn't quite strong enough. Here's some ointment for her incision. I'm not sure how you're traveling, but I'd recommend she get a lot of rest, whether it be in the car or wherever.'' She gave him complete instructions on her medicines and reminded him to examine her forehead and the incision from her back surgery every day.

''Thanks for understanding,'' Sam said, offering his hand.

''I hope you find her daughter safe and healthy.''

Sam didn't even want to consider the alternatives. He wouldn't. They would find Amy, and soon.

Six hours later, Sam helped Jessica into the hotel and knocked on Becky's door. ''Sorry to bother you.''

"How's she doing?"

"Much better," he said, as Becky pulled down the covers for Jessica, who sat down as soon as she saw the bed.

"What happened to her forehead?" Becky asked while Jessica reclined, pulling the covers over her.

"She fell into your plate when she passed out, and cut her head on your fork."

Becky covered her mouth to keep from laughing. "This can't all be happening to one person."

"Sometimes life just isn't fair," he said as he gave Jessica a good-night kiss.

She rolled over and snuggled the extra pillow without a word.

Sam walked into the hall with Becky following. "What's new?"

"I hoped you'd forget to ask," she said, brushing her hair off her face. "Deanne never got back onto the bus in Flagstaff."

Sam dropped back against the wall. "You're kidding me."

"Nope. She tried to rent a car—but without a credit card, they wouldn't rent her one. The rental company called the number on their system's message alert. He didn't tell her why her card was denied, but the Flagstaff police couldn't get there in time. I don't know if she's hiding out until her friend can pick her up, or if she'll resort to stealing a car..." Becky let out a deep breath.

Sam raked his hands through his hair and rubbed his face. "Did you call Jake? Maybe he can find new information."

"He doesn't have anything more."

Sam jammed his hands into his pockets and whispered a prayer. ''What now? She won't panic and hurt Amy, will she?''

Becky shrugged. ''Not likely if she loves her, but fear can make sick people do unpredictable things. Why don't we get some sleep? Whoever wakes first wakes the other. If you get a call, let me know.''

''If Jessica wakes up, let me know.''

''Is she up to the trip home, however long that takes?''

Sam updated her on the doctor's instructions and they both agreed to stay there one more day or until they had another lead on Deanne.

They didn't have long to wait, as the phone in Becky's room rang. Sam followed her back in, expecting the shrill noise to wake Jessica.

When Becky hung up, she said to Sam, ''Deanne was last seen getting into a white sedan with a businessman wearing a suit.''

''Traveling salesman?'' Sam suggested.

Becky stepped toward her bed. ''I hope he knows who his passengers are. Let's get a few hours of sleep and set a plan in the morning. Maybe we'll have another lead by then.''

Chapter Twenty

Jessica had about worn herself out trying to understand Sam. When he'd investigated Tim's accident, there had been no doubt that Sam disliked her. Now he was staying here, claiming he cared for her in a personal way. The way she had grown to care for him.

"You must be losing your mind," she whispered to herself, pacing the length of the small motel room, waiting for Becky to get back from the sheriff's office. She looked out the window at the green mountains and blue sky. Barely a wisp of white clouds rolled over the jagged peaks. *There's no way Sam and I could be in love,* she told herself. *Especially not in a matter of a few weeks.*

"Jessica, are you okay?"

She looked at Sam with wide eyes, imagining again that she heard something personal in his question. "I'm okay, considering. Why do you ask?"

He motioned at the bed. "You're not resting. What's wrong?"

She shrugged and turned away. "It's too quiet in here."

"Too quiet...as in, you want the television on?" He picked up the remote control.

"Don't!" She took it away and set it on the night-stand and looked into his eyes. "I guess that's not it, exactly. I can't stand to chance seeing another Amber Alert with Amy's picture on it."

Sam nodded. "You need to think of something besides Amy."

"I tried that, and this other topic brought up even more questions." Her gaze settled on Sam's whiskered jaw. They both looked a little ragged from hanging out in a motel waiting for the phone to ring.

Sam seemed to sense that she needed a hug, and he offered it generously. "I know this isn't easy. And I'm sorry we couldn't make it home last night. I didn't think we should drive until necessary. The doctor said..."

Jessica rested her head on his chest, comforted by his embrace. "I'm confused, Sam. And I'm ashamed of myself for even thinking of anything but Amy right now..." She looked at the heavily wooded forest just beyond the city limits and felt as if she were lost in the thick of it.

"It's okay, Jessi. She's one part of your life, but even now, you need to try to keep a balance. What are you confused about? Maybe I can help." He loosened the embrace and eased her away.

Jessica remembered the kiss he'd given her at the Broadmoor Hotel. And the few they had shared in the last week. Were they really in love, or was the attraction simply a distraction from the fear? An attempt to comfort each other? "I hope you can, because it's about you. Is this..." What a stupid question, she thought as she stepped away from his embrace. Cops didn't just go around hugging victims to make them feel better. They didn't stay on cases that were assigned to someone else.

"Is this what?"

"Between us… I'm confused. After Tim's accident, it was clear that you hated me."

"I didn't hate you." Sam furrowed his brow.

"You kept trying to blame me."

Sam edged away. "I felt you were trying to hide his drinking that night. I came down harder on you than I should have, probably, because Travis's wife and daughter were killed by a drunk boater. I admit, I have little patience for women who make excuses and stay in abusive relationships."

"So now, that leaves us…where?"

"What do you mean?"

"I was that woman, Sam. I won't deny it anymore." She took a deep breath, trying to regain her courage. She trusted Sam. Cared for him, more than she dared admit. "If I tell you everything, where will that leave our relationship?"

Sam's expression shifted from hopeful to somber. "Probably right where it's at right now. I think I've already figured out what happened, but I would like to know you trust me enough to tell me straight out."

Jessica couldn't believe that Sam had suspected anything near the truth and still thought he could love her. "Should we sit down?"

"If you want, go ahead. I'm fine."

Jessica wasn't about to trap herself in a chair if he wasn't. "I already told you about hiding money from him. It wasn't totally unjustified of him to restrict the bank account." She saw him roll his eyes. "I'm not making excuses for Tim. I'd started school without telling him. That wasn't right. But I knew I didn't want to leave Colorado Springs, even if he was stationed anywhere else. And I knew that we couldn't afford two residences. So I wanted to finish my degree and be ready to find a job. He found out, and wanted me to stay home with Amy and just be a mother.''

She wondered if Sam would comment, but he simply waited for her to continue. "He wasn't abusive unless he'd been drinking. Otherwise, he was a good father. We had been trying for another child, even though our marriage wasn't wonderful. I don't believe divorce should be an easy answer to problems between husband and wife. I was trying to do what I thought would keep him home more, as much as is possible in the military, anyway. Tim had one beer that night, early, before dinner.''

"Wait," Sam said, pacing the room. "What exactly were you doing to try to make him happy? Just being together wasn't enough?''

She shrugged. She knew he could never understand. Jessica couldn't look at Sam and tell him this part. "We hadn't been as close since Amy was born. I'd gained a lot of weight, and felt like if I could just do something different... And he'd been so attentive to me when I was pregnant, I suggested we have another baby. And things got better for a while. He didn't drink as much, stayed home more. I'd just found out I was pregnant before he came home from that last assignment. He wanted to go out, I wanted to stay home and tell him. He wasn't drunk. Drinking wasn't the reason he had the accident. I was. I made him leave the party before he had a chance to get drunk, and that made him mad. When we got in the car and headed home he was yell-ing. I told him to make a choice—drinking…or Amy and me.''

Sam said nothing for the longest while. Then he murmured, ''I'm proud of you for standing up to him, Jessi.''

Jessica wiped the tears from her cheek and looked away. ''If I had just waited until we got home, we wouldn't be here now. He slapped me, but that was the first time he'd ever touched me in anger. He hit a patch of black ice and…you know the rest.''

Sam crossed his arms over his chest and looked outside.

''You hug me, you call me Jessi, and yet you back away. You won't completely leave this search, but…''

He looked at the space between them and stepped closer. ''So you're confused by my behavior? You want to know what's happening between us on a personal note? So do I.''

Jessica hugged herself. ''I've heard that relationships born under duress don't stand a chance in lasting.''

''Odds were against you and Amy living through that accident, too. God has bigger plans for your life than to be a statistic, Jessi. You know as well as I do that a relationship is what you make it. And if there's one strength I have, it's that I never step back from a challenge. What you just told me changes everything between us. It makes me love you even more. It cost you your husband and a child. I'm guessing that you miscarried.''

She nodded.

''I didn't ever see mention of that in your file. I never suspected. I'm sorry for all you've had to go through. It makes me angry that you stayed in a marriage for all of the wrong reasons, yet at the same time I admire you even more because you were determined to keep your family together. And it infuriates me that Tim didn't value you enough to support your desire to further your education, whatever your reason for wanting it.''

Jessica felt the warmth of his embrace instinctively, before he was close enough to touch. She had always wondered what it would be like to have a man in her life who supported her despite her mistakes. Her parents had tried to tell her that she deserved better than Tim, yet she hadn't listened. And despite her mistakes, when she needed them, they had come and taken care of her. They had begged her to find a church again, where she could learn about God's love. *Thank You for loving me, God. And for giving me the love of a good man like Sam.*

She wondered if Sam could weasel his way out of the next question. ''So what are the statistics on finding Amy after she's been gone for almost nine days?''

''Don't think about that.''

''I'm wondering just how likely we are to find Amy.'' She pushed herself from the comfort and protection of Sam's strong arms. ''I want the facts, Sam.''

Sam looked into her bright gray eyes, wishing he had half the courage she had. She kept asking the question, and he was so cowardly, he couldn't answer. ''You don't want to know, and I sure don't want to tell you. We won't give up until we find her.''

''Becky got a call last night. She's been gone all morning. What's happening?''

Sam knew God had to have sent Jessica to him; she read him like an open book. She challenged him like no other woman ever had, and, like him, she was a fighter. ''I thought you were asleep when she got that call.''

She looked confused. "Was I?" Then she smiled. "I've had two good nights of sleep since this happened, and no matter how potent the drug, nothing's going to change until Amy's here with us."

Sam nodded in understanding. He couldn't argue that. "You need to get more rest so you don't end up in the hospital again."

"I'm going to be fine. Just like it says in Isaiah, 'When you pass through deep waters, I will be with you: your troubles will not overwhelm you.' If anyone should understand what deep water I've been under, it's Isaiah."

"If you think Isaiah had a rough life, you should read Job."

Jessica sat on the bed and reached for the drawer. "If we don't get out of here soon, I probably will." She lifted the complimentary Bible from the bedside table. "So if we're to trust God, and turn our lives over to Him, how is letting God be a crutch a bad thing?"

Sam sat on the other bed facing her. "God gives us gifts. We can't ignore the skills and abilities that He gave us while we wait for Him to answer our prayers."

She thought a moment. "But doesn't it say some-where that when we don't have the strength to stand on our own, God will sustain us, or carry us, or something like that? You know, like in that 'Footprints in the Sand' poem."

"Metaphorically, yeah, He carries us, but logically, God gives us the hope and faith to get through difficult times."

"But a crutch is something to lean on until you have the strength back for your legs to carry you on your own. They don't do the work for you, like a wheelchair does."

Sam thought a moment, then agreed. "Yeah, I see your point."

"So it's okay if I use God as my crutch to get through this ordeal?"

"Fine," he said with a smile. "We will get through this, and move on with life."

Jessica sighed. "Will I always live in fear of losing people I love, Sam? Is being a Christian like this, one test after another?"

"It's not without challenges. Like my mom says, having a baby is painful, but you're so focused on the new child afterward that usually women forget the intensity of pain."

Jessica laughed. "Believing in God is like having a baby?"

"Sure. Life gets pretty miserable, and if you don't know God as your Lord and Savior, what is there to look forward to? After you give your life to Christ, which some people consider a 'rebirth,' you have eternal life. After the baby is born, doesn't life look brighter through a child's simple joys?"

She looked as if she'd drifted away from him. "Most days, yeah. There will be a lot more joy when she's back home."

"Most days, being a Christian is pretty joyful. Days like this we realize how God humbled Himself when He came down to earth. He gave His child so we can have eternal life. God wept, just like we do. He didn't give His son a privileged life, He lived with the commoners. His friends betrayed Him, yet He continued to love, even His enemies."

She thought a moment. "I don't think I can be that forgiving of Deanne. So if that means—"

"Life is full of tests for all of us. I'm not a patient

man, and I've been reminded several times this past
month that life is not under my control, but His. All my
life I've had this image of the woman I'd marry. I've
prayed that God would let me know when I've really
found the right woman.''

Sam looked at the smile on her lips, the blush on her
face, and he knew, as sure as he knew Jesus had died
for his sins, that he'd found the love of his life.

''And I've wished that the next time I fall in love, it
would be with a really good man who doesn't care
about all of my mistakes.''

The phone trilled, startling both of them from the
emotional bond that had intensified between them in the
past hour.

''Detective Vance.''

''Is Detective Hilliard there yet? This is Sheriff Col-
lins. She left here a few minutes ago, but she needs to
call the Colorado Springs police station.''

Sam needed to be careful not to raise Jessica's hopes.
''Sure, I'll have Becky call them as soon as she gets
here. Any other message?''

''You'll want to start packing your bags, Detective.
The FBI agent in Santa Fe is setting up stakeouts at a
couple of hotels, trying to locate a woman and a little
girl. We don't have a positive ID on Jones yet.''

Sam could see the anticipation in Jessica's eyes, and
hesitated to ask more with her in the room. ''Who made
the report?''

''An eyeglass salesman gave a woman and a little
girl a ride from Flagstaff to Albuquerque. The woman
claimed to be Annabelle, and insisted on sitting in the
back seat with her daughter. He said they both slept a
fair amount of the trip. She said she could get a bus to
Santa Fe, where she had a job waiting. He didn't hear

the Amber Alert until the day after he'd dropped her off. The FBI agent verified that a woman and a little girl boarded the bus, but only had enough money to get to Santa Fe. She wanted to get to Colorado."

Sam felt a chill run up his spine. Jessica had said they were on their way home. "And they fit the description?"

"Not exactly—this little girl is brunette, and the woman has longer hair. Probably bought a wig to help hide her scars."

Sam reached for a pad of paper and took the pen from his shirt pocket. "Who's the FBI agent?" He scribbled the name and phone number. Since he dealt with major crimes, he hadn't worked with this agent yet. "What's the fastest route?"

"Take Highway 24 South, which is just past the hot springs. Stay on 84 through Chama, where the highway makes a turn right. Stay on that clear into Santa Fe. It's a three- to four-hour drive under normal circumstances. I'll let the New Mexico State Patrol know what you're driving. You shouldn't have any delays."

"Thanks, Sheriff. Do you still need Becky to call?" Sam leaned toward the phone, anxious to get moving.

"That about covers it. Good luck, and be careful down there."

When Sam turned around, Jessica was already packing and cleaning up. "Where are they?"

Sam touched her shoulder. "Don't get your heart set on this, Jessi. It might be them. Might not. The woman traveler had long brown hair, and the child has brown hair, too."

Jessica looked puzzled. "Brown hair? Amy has

brown hair? And Deanne's scar—how could anyone miss that?''

"Settle down, honey. We don't have all the answers yet. But we're about to get them.''

Chapter Twenty-One

Sam and Becky discussed the sheriff's call and agreed that Sam would drive so that Becky could coordinate plans with the FBI. Ten minutes after Becky arrived, they were on the road.

"Are you comfortable, Jessica?" Becky asked. "Have your water?"

"Don't worry about me, let's just get there and find Amy."

Sam looked at Becky. "Before you say anything, yes, I've made it clear that they aren't sure this is Deanne and Amy. And, Jessica, we may have another day of waiting, even if it is them. We'll have to assess the situation, make sure both of them are okay, what the conditions are, figure out any possible escape routes..." He paused, not wanting to tell her that she couldn't be anywhere nearby. "Why don't you try to sleep?"

"Not a chance. I don't want to miss anything."

Sam didn't bother trying to argue with her. There would be enough to disagree about when he dropped her off at the hotel.

Despite her attempts to stay awake, Jessica dozed again, and before long, they had arrived in the capital city of New Mexico. "There's our hotel. I'm meeting the FBI agent in the restaurant. Why don't you get Jessica settled, then meet us. He'll take us where we need to go."

Becky checked them into their rooms in the City Center Hotel and brought a set of key cards to Sam. He woke Jessica, and carried essential bags inside, leaving his own and Becky's for later. "Jessica, this way." He lifted the strap of her bag to his shoulder and took her hand. "We're on the fourth floor." She maneuvered the stairs fine, though she looked like a walking zombie, yawning, as if exhaustion had finally taken over.

"Is Amy here?" she said, yawning again.

"I don't know," he admitted, thankful that he didn't know more right now. "I'm meeting Becky and the FBI agent downstairs. So I need to get you into the room and comfortable."

"But I want to see if it's Amy."

Sam reached their room and unlocked the door. He set the bags down, then coaxed her inside with him. "You can't come with us this time, honey."

"But…"

He placed a finger over her lips. "This is a federal investigation now. I'm sure the agent will need to talk to you, and I want you to stay in here in case we need to reach you. Okay?" Their eyes met and he could see the fear hiding behind her brave facade.

She spun away. "I slept on the way here. If I just go with you now, the FBI can talk to me right away."

"We aren't in charge of this case anymore. You'll be safer in here."

Jessica turned pale and dropped onto the bed. "You

think Deanne is dangerous now? Why? What makes you think that?"

Sam shook his head. He wanted to be patient with her, but he had to get going or he wouldn't know what was happening. "I don't know, Jessi. But I do need to go find Amy, and I can't do that if I'm worried about you." He knelt in front of her and kissed her trembling lips. "She's not at this hotel, so we need to coordinate with the FBI." He noticed the time and felt an urgency to leave. "I need you to promise me you'll take your medicine again and try to sleep. Trust me, Jessica. I'll be back as soon as I can."

"With Amy." She smiled, following him to the door. "You'll find Amy and bring her here to me."

If it's Amy, he thought. He opened the door and stepped through it, then turned back for another kiss. "Yeah, I'll bring Amy back to you. Take your medicine."

"You go on, I'll find it."

Could he trust her? "I don't want to be worried about you. Amy's going to be so happy to see you, we won't be able to get either of you to sleep. You need to rest now, if for no other reason than to make time go faster."

He realized he'd probably gone too far when Jessica started crying. "You'd better hurry, and Sam, be careful."

Sam closed the door behind him and listened to the latch click echo off the adobe veranda. He ran down the stairs and looked up to their room from the courtyard below.

"Sam, we're over here," Becky said quietly from over the flower-covered adobe wall. Piñon trees and small yucca cacti created a privacy wall on the other side.

He looked up to their room again, then ducked under the canvas umbrella. "What are you doing out here?"

She placed her pointer finger over her mouth. "Things are moving a little quicker than we thought they would," she whispered. "They're in the corner room, first floor."

Sam fought the urge to turn around and look.

She explained a phone call the police had received from a motel manager alerting them to a suspicious woman and child. "The police recognized the description, and contacted area hotels to tell her the credit card had cleared, and to call them right away. That happened about an hour into our drive. They tried to call us, but we must have been in a dead area. I didn't realize I had a message."

"So are we sure it's them?" Sam asked, noting how close the agent and Becky were sitting. He realized they were posing as a couple having a drink before dinner.

Sam had to laugh at seeing Becky with a long-haired agent. The middle-aged man introduced himself; he seemed to be enjoying the cover assignment. "Amy tugged on the wig and almost pulled it off. Jones lost her temper and spun around, and the clerk was able to identify Deanne's scars," he added. "We're just waiting on the city police to set the perimeter."

Sam had nearly gotten lost in the Plaza downtown in the center of town. He could understand why it was taking so long to contain the area without raising Deanne's suspicions. Behind them the cathedral bells rang at the top of the hour. Sam closed his eyes, asking God's protection and favor to recover Amy without anyone getting hurt.

The agent whispered something into Becky's ear, and she giggled.

"You two want me to leave? I'd hate to blow your cover." Without thinking, Sam flipped his badge from outside his belt to inside his waistband. He hoped no one had noticed already.

Becky smiled. "Just sit down, you…" She looked at the sliding glass door in the corner.

Sam turned, catching a glimpse of Amy. He'd recognize those eyes anywhere. They were almond shaped, just like her mother's. He took a small step behind the scraggly pine, hoping to catch a glimpse inside the room. "It's Amy."

"Hang tight," the FBI agent instructed quietly, separating himself from Becky, trying to move the wrought-iron chairs without making any noise on the concrete slab.

Amy pressed her nose to the glass, then turned and looked behind her. She inched her hand for the door latch, obviously keeping watch for Deanne.

"That's it, Amy, unlock the door. Quiet," Sam whispered.

Becky scolded him. "She can't hear you."

Sam ignored her. "Mommy's waiting upstairs for you, Amy. Come out to Sam." He peeked through the tree. "God, help her escape unharmed."

"Let's move."

"No," Sam ordered. "Amy sees you two running toward her, you never know what she may do. Let's see if she makes it."

Amy peeked out of the curtains again, pressed both of her hands against the glass and pushed.

The door opened a few inches, and Amy stepped out, pausing for a second. They all hesitated, as if waiting for Deanne to snatch her back inside. Amy turned back, reached inside the room, then ran for the pool, and Sam took off running toward her.

"Amy," he said quietly to steal her attention away from the water.

She looked up at him and smiled. "Thammy." She turned toward him and ran into his arms, just as Deanne called her name.

Sam glanced over at the table and noticed it was empty. He couldn't see anyone around. He thought of pulling the gun from his back, but prayed that the other two had him covered. She bolted out of the room, wearing jeans and a baggy sweatshirt, where she could have anything hidden. Since it had taken her five hours to make her way to this hotel, suspicion was high that she'd found either help or a gun. The last hotel clerk may have unknowingly tipped her off.

"Hi, I saw her headed toward the pool. Since I didn't see an adult, I…"

Deanne looked at him suspiciously. "I went to the bathroom for a second—" She cursed and stepped toward Sam with outstretched arms. "I'll take her now."

Sam backed away, seeing Becky and the agent pulling their weapons. "Deanne Jones, you're under arrest. Put your hands on your head," the FBI agent said.

Deanne recognized Sam now, and started running. Sam took cover behind the adobe wall with Amy in his arms, glad to let the others take off after Deanne. He took several deep breaths, trying to regain a normal tone for Amy's sake. "Hi, Amy. Where's your bear?"

"Boo." She produced it from in-between them. Funny how he hadn't noticed her even carrying it. She hugged the ratty bear to her chest and looked as if she could squeeze the stuffing out the toes.

He brushed the hair from her face. "Are you okay?"

She scrunched her face and growled. "No, no, Amy," she muttered, along with a long story that sounded like a record playing in fast speed. She wrapped her arms around Sam's neck and held tight. "Not-ee Dee."

"Deanne was naughty, wasn't she." He heard shots fired, and pulled Amy closer. "Want to go see Mommy?" Surely Becky would know where to find them.

Amy jumped in his arms and her eyes brightened from beneath her brown bangs. "Mama, Mama," she chanted, wiggling with excitement.

Hopefully this was the end of a very long ordeal for Jessica and Amy, and right now he prayed that Jessica didn't hear those gunshots over the air-conditioning.

Chapter Twenty-Two

Sam opened the door, surprised to find Jessica asleep on the bed. Amy smiled. "Shhh, Mommy's sleeping."

"Yes, she is." His heart swelled. She had trusted him, not once, or twice, but three times now to care for her daughter, whom she loved more than anyone. He kissed Amy's cheek and knelt on the floor. "Go give Mommy a kiss. Be careful of her back remember."

Amy nodded. "Owie." She handed Sam her bear, then climbed onto the bed next to Jessica and laid her head on the pillow. "Mommy, owie." She gently touched the bandage on Jessica's forehead, then kissed it. Laying nose to nose, Amy patted Jessica's cheek. "Mommy tired."

"Yes, she is. You can take a nap with her if you'd like to." Amy reached her chubby little hand and motioned "some." Sam realized he was holding her bear and handed it to her. She tucked it between them and closed her eyes.

Sam inched the door open and stepped outside to call Becky. If she could, she'd answer. If not, this wasn't over despite the sirens wailing closer. He dialed and waited. On the fifth ring, Becky answered. "Hey there."

"Becky? Are you okay?"

"It's just a scratch on the head."

"She shot you in the head?"

Becky laughed. "Not a chance. I shot her, then ran into a hanging pot of flowers. The paperwork is going to take a while on this one. She'll make it, but it's going to be a while before she's on her feet again."

"If you need help, maybe the FBI can help. I'm going to have my hands full here."

"How are they? Is Jessica crying yet?"

"She took her pain medicine, and it's finally knocked her out. Amy—" Sam's voice gave out and tears blurred his vision.

"I never thought I'd hear Sam Vance choked up."

"You'd better keep it to yourself, or the entire department will be hearing about the long-haired narc that you were cozy undercover with."

She laughed. "Well, you know, not everyone can get away with long hair like he can. He probably even looks good with short hair. When Jessica wakes up, give me a call. I'll have a car pick you up. In the meantime, get some rest and enjoy your new family."

"Who said anything about that?"

"You didn't have to say a word, it's written all over both of you." Sam heard the sirens warble to a halt. "Hey, my ride's here, I'll catch you later."

Sam stepped inside, relieved to find both Mathers females sleeping soundly. He looked at the other bed, tempted to take a nap himself. Finding nowhere to lock up his weapon, he opted for ordering dinner instead. When room service knocked on the door, Jessica stirred.

"Amy," she mumbled. Her hand landed on Amy's fine strands of hair and she woke up instantly. "Oh God, thank you, God."

"Mommy," Amy wrapped her arms around Jessica's neck. They snuggled and kissed.

"Oh, Amy."

Sam found chairs to pull up to the table and uncovered the plates. "Hey ladies, dinner's on."

Jessica looked at Sam with tears in her eyes. "Thank you."

"Any time." All the time, he should have said. He wasn't about to leave their safety to anyone else. "We have a lot to do tonight, paperwork, interviews with the news…"

She and Amy washed up for dinner and sat down. "You'll be there with us, right?"

"Yeah, Colleen Montgomery called with her congratulations. She wants an exclusive interview tomorrow. I think we'd better tell her to take my name off the bachelor auction."

Jessica looked at him, puzzled. "Why?"

"I'm no longer available."

She smiled. "You really think you can take us for another month?"

"I was thinking a lifetime."

The smile softened. "I think we should give it some time. You know how I feel about statistics."

"And you know how I feel about beating the odds. Take all the time you need to answer, but regardless—"

Jessica stepped next to him and gave him an unforgettable kiss, stopping his words.

He continued. "There are a few arrangements I'd like you to consider."

Amy climbed into the chair and into Sam's arms. "My daddy?"

Jessica laughed. "That didn't take long."

Sam gave her his best smile, hugging Amy's face next to his. "Surely you couldn't turn us both down."

She took both of them into her arms and kissed each one. "I love you two more than I ever thought imaginable. But I'm not sure a woman on medication should make life-altering decisions. Why don't we say a prayer before she devours everything?" They all sat down and Jessica showed Amy how to fold her hands to pray. Jessica started the prayer with praise, and Sam ended with thanks.

Sam realized that it had been almost ten hours since he and Jessica had eaten, and who knows how long since Amy had.

Jessica's cell phone rang, and she dug through her purse to answer it. "Hi, Mom. Where are you?"

Sam set Amy in her own chair and they both started eating. Jessica paced the suite, glancing at them every few minutes. She had a healthy glow back, along with that beautiful twinkle in her gray eyes. And this time, it wasn't tears. She smiled, then bit her lower lip.

"Sam, my dad wants to talk to you."

He looked at her surprised. "Me?" he whispered. "Why?"

She nodded. "They want to thank their future son-in-law."

He'd never understood women, and Jessica topped the list. One minute she wanted to wait, the next, she was ready to get married.

She tucked the phone behind her back and leaned

close. "They don't know about us yet. You might want to ask them to meet us for dinner tomorrow night."

"From Italy?"

"They're in Colorado Springs. They just heard the news that we found Amy. Nothing would make them happier than to see Amy and I in such caring hands."

Sam paused to give Jessica a thorough kiss as he tried to pry the phone from her hands. "What's your dad's name?" Jessica simply smiled and bit into her chicken. "Hello, sir. This is Sam Vance."

"Donald Owens, Jessica's father. I understand you've found our granddaughter again. I'm also told that you've been taking care of Jessi through this ordeal." His voice gave out. "We can't thank you enough, Detective. We worry so much about Jessica. We couldn't take it another day, not knowing how they were doing."

Sam listened with closed eyes, trying to imagine what her parents would look like. He already liked her dad. Who couldn't like a dad who would fly all the way from Italy to take care of his daughter? "I can't take credit for actually finding Amy this time, Mr. Owens. But I couldn't be happier that we have a happy ending." They talked for a while longer, until Jessica's phone beeped, indicating a low battery. "We'll see you tomorrow."

Jessica and Amy had finished eating, and waited at the table patiently for Sam to eat. "So, are we getting together tomorrow?"

Sam wondered for a moment if he should listen to Jessica, and give life a chance to settle down before pushing for marriage.

Jessica mentioned calling a real-estate agent while her parents were here to look at houses and help her with Amy. "I've probably missed the one we were waiting on, but surely it's not the only town house available in our price range. Maybe you could look at them with me, tell me if it's a good neighborhood for Amy."

"Why are you looking at houses if we're talking about marriage? Unless you didn't like my house. In which case, we can find something together."

She looked startled. "My landlord sold the house, and the new owner doesn't want renters. I have to be out next month. I missed the one town house because of the kidnapping, which may be a blessing, but I'll need someplace to live until we get married, even if it's a rental."

He nodded, thinking about how ridiculous it was for her to move twice. "Why don't you and Amy live in my house, and I'll stay with my parents? Or I'm sure Travis wouldn't mind if I stayed in his basement for a few weeks."

"Weeks? Mom and Dad probably can't come back again before summer. If then. Finding substitutes in Italy who can teach American students isn't very easy." She explained the ordeal they had gone through to find suitable replacements for their short visit.

"How long were you planning to wait to get married?"

"Well, I was thinking July, until Mom and Dad showed up. Now, I'm not sure."

Sam shook his head. "Jessi," he looked at Amy and smiled. "What do you think about moving it up a few months? Amy's just gone through such a traumatic experience, and you need to move, and your parents are already here, and I've already admitted that I'm not terribly patient when I know what I want."

She looked at him, startled. "But, you know so little

about me, and I just think you should give it more time.''

"I notice you don't seem concerned with knowing so little about me. Why does that not concern you?'' He leaned across the table and smiled. "Or should I ask my mother that question?''

Jessica laughed, and Amy imitated her. "I know that Pastor Gabriel told us that another person can't fulfill us, but I question that. I can't explain how much different I feel when I'm with you, Sam. Even when I've been mad at you, I have no doubts that you're listening to more than just my words. You aren't like the other men I've met since Tim died. I have no doubts about my feelings for you, but I want you to be sure…''

"I'm absolutely certain about my feelings, Jessica. I dated Becky for almost three years, and never felt the kind of connection we have. Before Becky, there were a few steady girlfriends. I'm old enough to know what I'm feeling, and that I don't want to look anywhere else. God has answered my prayers over and over. I want you and Amy in my life forever.''

"It was only a few hours ago that I told you about my marriage, Sam. You haven't even had a chance to think about it. How about if we sleep on the idea this week? We'll keep it kind of quiet, see each other when we can, and talk about it later.''

Sam knew a week wouldn't make any difference to him, but figured it would ease Jessica's insecurities. She'd rushed into marriage with Tim and regretted it. If a few more days would convince her that his feelings weren't going to change, he'd go along with it.

The week hadn't gone at all as planned. He and Jessica had met with her parents for dinner, but other than that, they hadn't had a minute together. He called Saturday morning to arrange to pick Jessica up for the Darling-Montgomery wedding. Her parents had already made other plans for the day.

Jessica had spent all morning curling Amy's hair for the occasion. Monday afternoon her hairdresser had been able to get Amy's hair color back to her normal blond. She wanted Amy to look like herself, not the victim Deanne had taken. Between doctor's appointments for herself and Amy, she'd gone to work very little. Her parents had taken care of Amy while she was out, and enjoyed every minute of it.

It had been a long week without seeing Sam or his family, and Jessica was surprised to feel the butterflies in her stomach at the thought. They had taken such good care of her, yet she was no longer the emotional mess she had been. Would they like the real Jessica Mathers?

Sam looked like a prince in the black tuxedo. Amy, who still wasn't up to speed with most three-year-old conversationalists, looked at him and said, "Pretty Daddy." Jessica laughed. "Sam looks very handsome, doesn't he? Boys look handsome, girls look pretty," she reminded her daughter. Sam kissed Jessica hungrily and then picked Amy up.

"And you girls look even more than pretty. You both look beautiful."

Jessica and Amy sat with the Vance family. She loved listening to and watching Sam play the keyboard. It was like a concert of love songs, and she imagined he was singing every one to her.

Kate made a stunning bride, and Adam didn't let a moment go by without noticing that fact. Every detail of the wedding had been perfect from the twinkle lights to the peach-colored rose petals scattered down the aisle. After the ceremony, they all drove across town to the Broadmoor Hotel. The pink stucco resort looked as majestic and regal as always. Jessica found herself paying attention to little details that a month ago had gone totally unnoticed. Things like how Kate's earrings matched her necklace, and the sparkles in the hotel's granite driveway glistened almost as much as the bride's diamond. She and Adam beamed.

Jessica realized that they, too, had had a whirlwind romance, and a short-notice wedding. What was it about this group of friends? Had they simply realized their clocks were ticking? Had God opened their eyes to the beauty of love? Or was it something about the state of society that had all of them impatient to get to the altar?

Sam took Jessica into his embrace and swayed to the violin music. "Are you gathering ideas?"

She blushed. "Maybe, though I'm sure the Broadmoor is out of the question for us."

"That's fine with me. Just so we're married at the end of our wedding day, it doesn't matter if the wedding is large or small, fancy or simple. What would you like?"

"Would you mind something small? Just close friends and family? These fancy weddings are gorgeous, but I'm not very comfortable with all this glitz."

"I'm fine if you just want to have Judge Warren meet us in his quarters."

She and Sam walked hand in hand, visiting about their own wedding, as if the subject were public knowledge. Jessica watched Amy carefully, giving her only as much freedom as possible, seeing as they'd only recovered her five days ago.

"The fall colors are so pretty, what would you think of an outdoor wedding?"

"Fall, as in next month, or next year?"

"Mom and Dad's return flight is September twelfth. Think we could fit it into our schedules before then? Unless you've decided I'm not quite what you had in mind after all?" Sam's tasty answer soundly denied that he'd changed his mind. She felt the heat into the pit of her stomach.

His kisses still left her light-headed. "Does that answer your ridiculous question?" He released Jessica, and she smiled, then noticed Amy.

"Amy, get back up here. You don't want to get your pretty dress dirty."

"Me go fwiming."

Jessica watched in horror as her meticulously primped daughter dipped her patent leather shoe into the pond. "No, Amy! Get up here, right now."

"She won't do it, will she?" Sam asked as Jessica rushed across the grass to the lake.

Amy dropped to her hands and knees and backed right into the water. Jessica stepped to the edge of the shore and reached in after her. Amy floated away, showing off her newly learned swimming skills. "Amy!" Jessica slipped off her own shoes and stepped into the pond after her, walking almost four feet from the shore before she was able to latch on to her slippery fingers and pull Amy to shore. "Amy, why did you do that? You're not dressed for swimming."

One of the hotel staff arrived with several towels. "Is she okay?"

"Yes, she's fine, just wanted to go swimming. I'm sorry for the inconvenience." Jessica turned bright pink. "Oh, Sam, I'm so sorry. How embarrassing."

"Amy fwim," she said, stubbornly trying to enunciate, while backing away from Jessica's embrace. She wasn't supposed to lift anything over twenty pounds yet, and Amy far exceeded that.

"Nope, Amy's going home and straight to her room." Jessica insisted before realizing she'd ridden here with Sam and his parents. Sam wrapped her in a towel and lifted her into his arms.

"Amy," he said gently but firmly. He waited until she stopped fighting him. "Swimming in your pretty dresses is a no-no. And you need to listen when your Mommy tells you no."

"No," she said, sticking her chin out.

Jessica could have died. She wanted nothing more than to go home to her tiny apartment with child locks on the cabinets and door locks six feet off the floor. Sam would surely change his mind now. Not only did his future stepchild look like a ragamuffin, but so did his fiancée. She had mud up to her knees, and the bottom three inches of her dress dripped steadily.

Sam carried Amy to a secluded corner away from the party and held her as she cried herself to sleep. Jessica carried the extra towels in one hand and her sandals in the other. "Her schedule is still off," Jessica said as she joined Sam and sat down.

"No one deserves this more than Sam," Lidia said with a laugh, coming up from behind them. "We brought the kids here for the fireworks one year, and he and Jake Montgomery both ended up in Cheyenne Lake."

Sam shrugged, as if he could have forgotten that one. "I was five, and he was chasing me with a crawdad."

Jessica looked at the man she loved and tried to imagine him running from anything.

Colleen Montgomery turned from the table next to

them. "I seem to remember Sammy giving me a gift once, a frog in my lunch box."

"You *liked* frogs."

"Not in my lunch box." Colleen looked at Jessica and smiled. "Don't worry, Jessica, the managers here are prepared for anything when our families walk through those doors. Looks like the next generation is ready to follow suit."

Chapter Twenty-Three

By the time Sam dropped them off, Jessica's sides hurt from the unbelievable stories she'd heard about her husband-to-be's childhood antics.

She and Sam hadn't seen each other all week. Partly to give each other space, and mostly because they both had so much to do to catch up at work. They had seen each other once since they'd returned, to finish filling out the reports on Amy's case.

Deanne had been moved from a New Mexico hospital to a mental hospital in Colorado. Though Jessica had Amy at home with her, she knew they had a long, messy trial ahead. It would be months before she'd feel safe again.

To begin her own journey of healing, Jessica knew she would feel better with Amy away from the shelter. She'd interviewed and hired a licensed child-care provider who watched five children in her home. She had glowing recommendations from parents, and the home was still close to the shelter.

Sam had finally convinced her to drop the idea of

finding an apartment. He wanted to know she and Amy were in a safe neighborhood, so they were moving Jessica and Amy into his house and he was moving temporarily to his parents'.

Jessica packed the pictures of Deanne and Amy into a box to stay in storage. She couldn't look at them yet, but one day, she might be ready.

"How's the packing coming along?" her dad asked, taping the box closed.

"Fine, Daddy. How was your trip to Cripple Creek?"

"Beautiful drive." He filled her in on their day. "So when do we get to spend some time with you and Sam?"

"Tomorrow. I have dinner planned at his house tomorrow evening. Chicken cordon bleu, your favorite."

"Sounds wonderful, honey." While they packed, Jessica told them all about the Darling-Montgomery wedding and Amy's introduction to the Vance family.

The next morning, Jessica directed her parents to the Good Shepherd Christian Church and introduced them to Sam's parents, who were just leaving after the earlier service.

"We'd love to have you join us for dinner today," Lidia said to them as the keyboard began playing inside.

Though Jessica had been generous with interviews during the week, she was surprised to hear Pastor Gabriel invite a journalist inside, and then call Sam, Jessica and Amy to the front. "This blessing shows the power of bringing community together in prayer. For the last two weeks, we prayed together for Amy's safe return, and today, I'm praising the Lord that both Amy and Jessica Mathers are here with us."

When the cheers quieted, Jessica stepped up to the

microphone. "I can't tell you how touched I was by the love I felt here after Amy's disappearance. I accepted God as my Savior, and through this past two weeks when I normally would have fallen to pieces, I know it was the grace of God holding me together, carrying me through the rough times and over the pits of despair. Thank you for your prayers, and I look forward to joining all of you in fellowship and prayers for a long time."

Amy saw Susan Carter and her friends Hannah and Sarah waving from the back of the room, and she waved back, then pushed herself from Sam's strong hold to run to sit with her grandparents. Jessica laughed. "As you can see, Amy is just fine." She paused and tears came to her eyes. "I'd ask that we pray for the kidnapper, Deanne Jones. I'm not going to pretend that I've overcome my anger enough to forgive her, but I am grateful that she didn't hurt Amy in any way."

Sam wrapped his arm around her and asked to be excused from leadership so that he could sit with Jessica and her family, bringing several smiles and even more raised eyebrows from friends and fellow worshipers.

When Sam and Jessica arrived at Max and Lidia's house, they were surprised to see Travis and Lucia. Even Sam's ex-sister-in-law, Emily Armstrong, his cousins, Michael and Holly Vance, and his Aunt Marilyn had come.

If Jessica's parents felt uncomfortable or overwhelmed, it wasn't obvious. Lidia enjoyed the chance to catch up on her native Italy with them, and Max seemed to find plenty to talk about with Jessica's father, Donald.

Before dinner was served, Sam was able to find time to speak privately with her parents. "Mr. and Mrs.

Owens, I apologize for the crowd and lack of privacy. I'd hoped to do this a little differently, but…''

"We feel right at home, Sam. Please, call us by our first names."

"Evelyn, Donald, as you're aware, I first met Jessica at the accident that killed her husband. When we met again a couple of weeks ago, it was more than fate bringing us together—it was as if God had been working overtime to open our eyes." He looked at them, his hands shaking and his voice threatening to give out. "The kidnapping gave Jessica and me a lot of time to be together, and…we've fallen in love. I'd like to ask your permission to marry Jessica."

"Do you know the meaning of the name Samuel?"

Sam looked at Evelyn, feeling more than a little puzzled. What did that have to do with his request? "No, I guess I don't."

She listed the prophet Samuel's lineage. "Hannah had been barren, and asked the Lord to bless her with a child to fill her heart. When she finally conceived, she named him Samuel because she'd asked the Lord for him. We've prayed that God would bless a man to love Jessica as much as we do."

"We would be honored to have you as a son, Samuel. I can't tell you how long it's been since we've seen such a beautiful smile on our daughter's face," Donald said, then offered his hand. "And what a comfort it will be to know that she'll have lots of family around, too."

After shaking his hand, Sam hugged Evelyn and thanked them for their blessing. "If you'll excuse me…"

Their smiles showed their approval. "Go ahead. When things quiet down, we'll visit."

"Oh, I should probably mention that we'd like to tie

the knot before you return to Italy." The Owens expressed their delight.

He found Jessica and Amy playing outside on the tire swing with his brother Travis. Travis saw Sam, and headed inside. "Need me to stall dinner for you?"

Sam laughed. "No, we shouldn't be very long."

Jessica looked up with a smile. "How'd it go?"

"If we want to make an official announcement we'd better hurry. Once word gets out here, it's as good as gospel." He reached into his pocket and pulled out a diamond solitaire. "Jessica, I can't imagine going through another week without you and Amy next to me. God has richly blessed us, and I know He'll continue to do so, if you'll be my wife."

She answered his proposal with a slow, thoughtful kiss. "I finally realized why you're in such a hurry to get married. It's not that you're impatient, you're just trying to get out of the bachelor auction."

Sam blushed. "Fine, we can wait until after the auction if you want—just so you understand, there's only one woman I'm taking on that date. Unless, of course, you'd like to look at it as a honeymoon package."

"I think it's going to be too late for that." She extended her hand to him and gazed at the brilliant diamond. "Sam, this is too much, you shouldn't have…"

"Ooh, pretty ring, Mommy."

Sam picked up Amy and leaned close to Jessica. "Beautiful, Jessica, simply beautiful. Just like you. This was my great-grandmother's ring."

They kissed again, a roar from inside the house cheering them on. Jessica glanced at the crowd gathering at the window, then looked up to Sam. "Okay, so you were right about that one. As long as they're in such a festive mood, maybe we should get started planning.''

Sam intertwined his fingers with hers. ''With this crowd, you're going to have no problem with just two weeks' notice.''

''Good. They can plan the wedding, we'll plan the honeymoon.''

* * * * *

Dear Reader,

Thank you for choosing to read *Finding Amy*. Hopefully you're enjoying the entire FAITH ON THE LINE series from Book One through Book Six. Writing this has been a great challenge, coordinating with other authors, attempting to portray our characters in the same image and telling a good story at the same time. *Finding Amy* will always be a special book to me. When the editors asked me to write it, I was thrilled to find out that it included all the things I know: cops, mothers, children (yes, I even have a personal relationship with back pain) and the challenge of loving and trusting God through crises. After fifteen years, and caring for over a hundred children, this book tested my writing skills. Talk about a true test! I hope that I've done the story justice and portrayed it realistically.

For those who would like to find out more about my writing, please visit my Web site at www.carolsteward.com.

In His Love,

Carol Steward

Jessica's friend and boss Susan Carter was a busy single mom with twin daughters and a shelter all depending on her. Love was something she wasn't looking for, until the new pastor came to town.

Look for her story in

GABRIEL'S DISCOVERY,

coming only to Love Inspired in September 2004.

For a sneak preview, please turn the page.

Chapter One

Laughing, Gabriel watched Susan's daughters race off, holding hands as they ran, long beaded braids flying out behind them. "Your daughters are a delight, Mrs. Carter."

"More like a handful," she said. "And why don't you call me Susan."

"I will," he said with a smile.

Susan spent a moment regretting that he wouldn't be one of the bachelors up for auction at the fund-raising gala the following weekend. Forget the fantasy dates Jessica had set up; she'd make a generous donation to her own cause just to watch this man smile.

"Only if you'll call me Gabriel."

"It's a deal," she said. "Though I'm not in the habit of calling clergy members by their first names."

"Then don't think of me as clergy."

She raised an eyebrow. "How am I supposed to accomplish that?" Like a game show hostess displaying the grand prize for correctly answering the bonus-round question, she swept her hand in front of her. "Look at this. We're at your church's annual Labor Day picnic. The church is right over there with your name displayed in rather *large* letters, I might say.''

Gabriel chuckled. ''I had nothing to do with that sign.''

A huge red-and-white banner welcomed members and friends to the church picnic. Gabriel's name was printed almost as big as the church's.

''Do you mind if we stroll that way? I want to keep an eye on the girls.'' She didn't wait for his answer, but started moving in the direction of the entertainer so that she could see Hannah and Sarah.

''They're identical,'' Gabriel said. ''How do you tell them apart?''

''I'm the mom, I'm supposed to.''

''I bet you get that question a lot with twins.''

Susan's answer got interrupted.

''Hey, Pastor Gabriel. Wait!'' The kettle-corn vendor ran around his booth with a big bag of the sweetly flavored popcorn in hand. ''Here you go. For you and your pretty lady.''

Susan flushed and found herself grateful that her dark skin concealed most of the blush. Gabriel glanced at her and smiled, but he didn't correct the concessionaire.

Instead he dug in his pocket for money, but the vendor shook his head.

''No charge, Pastor. We just want to thank you for letting us set up shop here this year. Business has been great all day. The missus and I are gonna come to one of your services this Sunday.''

''Glad to hear it,'' Gabriel said, shaking the man's hand. ''I'll look for you. And we're pleased to have you with us today. Thanks again.''

"Anytime, Reverend. Nice to meet you, ma'am," the vendor said to Susan, who simply smiled.

Gabriel offered the bag to Susan. She opened her mouth to ask why he hadn't disabused the man of the notion that they were a couple, then decided that to call attention to it would only be…what? More embarrassing? So instead of saying anything, she accepted some popcorn.

"Mmm. This is good." She looked back at the booth. The vendor waved and she waved back. "I'll have to remember to get some for the girls."

As they strolled across the lawn, several people called out to either Susan or Gabriel as they passed.

"You're quite a celebrity here," he said. "It seems like everyone knows you."

"Does that make you uncomfortable?"

He gave her an odd look, and Susan regretted the challenging tone she'd taken with him.

Then he smiled. "No. I like strong women."

Susan hid a grin by taking another nibble of popcorn.

"I'm actually glad you came over," she said. "I wanted to speak with you about something."

"Hi there, Pastor Gabriel," said a man who touched the brim of his Denver Broncos cap in greeting as he headed in the opposite direction. "Great picnic."

"Thanks, nice seeing you, John."

"You're the popular one," Susan observed.

Good Shepherd Christian Church's Labor Day picnic had grown into something of a tradition for members of the congregation as well as the community. The church stocked what seemed like an endless supply of hot dogs, hamburgers, chips and soft drinks. Picnic-goers could then purchase other treats, like kettle corn and cotton candy, or T-shirts and CDs from vendors set up on two sides of the church's lawn.

"New preacher giving away free food," Gabriel said. "What's not to like?"

Susan chuckled. "The hard times will come later, huh?"

"Like death and taxes. So, you said you wanted to speak with me about something."

Enjoying the light moments with him, Susan found herself reluctant to end the easy companionship, but she had business to tend to, business that directly involved Reverend Dawson.

He *was* popular and bright. That's why she didn't understand why in all his outreach efforts to date, he hadn't stopped by or inquired about Galilee.

"You've been here almost a year now," she said.

Gabriel nodded. "Nine months."

"You've done a lot in the community. I've seen your name on several boards and you've started a couple of outreach ministries."

He glanced at her. "I'm hearing a *but* coming."

Susan had the grace to smile. "But you've missed a big pocket of the community."

"And what pocket is that?"

"Women in need."

He looked at her then, wondering if he should read a dual message in her comment. "What, specifically, do you mean?"

"I'd like to show you our facility," she said. "Why don't you stop by the Galilee shelter and let me show you around?"

"You're still the director there, right?"

Susan nodded.

"I'd be glad to put it in my book," he told her. "I'll have Karen schedule it. Maybe I'll stop by in a couple of months. What I've been trying to do first is get a feel for the larger community, some of the broader issues that have the biggest impact not only on members of Good Shepherd, but on the people who live in the area that the church serves.''

Susan bristled at his implication that abused women didn't rank very high on his priority or impact list.

That was the problem she had with him. Her goal today was to get him to commit to visiting the shelter. She hoped that once he saw for himself the work that was done there, he'd make a long-term commitment to the shelter's mission.

Her job today was to waylay the good reverend and make him see the error of his neglectful ways—at least where Galilee Women's Shelter was concerned.

''Reverend Dawson, I think you'll change your mind when you see what we're doing at Galilee.''

''You're not going to stop until I say yes, are you.''

She lifted her hands in a ''it's your call'' gesture.

''All right, then. I will come by.''

Susan wanted to dance a jig. With the newest pastor in town also supporting the effort, maybe something could be done about the problems plaguing the city— in particular, areas near Good Shepherd.

She knew how to close a deal, too. ''How about tomorrow morning?''

Gabriel laughed. ''I have appointments all day.''

She looked doubtful.

''Really. I do,'' he said.

''Then what about…''

''How about Wednesday?'' he suggested. ''Ten o'clock?''

Susan's smile for him was bright. She caught herself before she said *It's a date.* ''I'll see you then.''

Love Inspired®

A HEART'S REFUGE

BY

CAROLYNE AARSEN

Rick Ethier couldn't refuse his grandfather's proposition: revive a faltering magazine and be free to pursue his own interests. The only obstacle was Becky Ellison, current editor—not a fan of Rick's since his negative review of her first book. Yet the restless Rick soon learned that the things he'd been longing for all his life—love, community, faith—were within his grasp…with Becky.

Don't miss

A HEART'S REFUGE

On sale September 2004

Available at your favorite retail outlet.

Take 2 inspirational love stories FREE!

PLUS get a FREE surprise gift!

Mail to Steeple Hill Reader Service™

In U.S.
3010 Walden Ave.
P.O. Box 1867
Buffalo, NY 14240-1867

In Canada
P.O. Box 609
Fort Erie, Ontario
L2A 5X3

YES! Please send me 2 free Love Inspired® novels and my free surprise gift. After receiving them, if I don't wish to receive anymore, I can return the shipping statement marked cancel. If I don't cancel, I will receive 4 brand-new novels every month, before they're available in stores! Bill me at the low price of $4.24 each in the U.S. and $4.74 each in Canada, plus 25¢ shipping and handling and applicable sales tax, if any*. That's the complete price and a savings of over 10% off the cover prices—quite a bargain! I understand that accepting the books and gift places me under no obligation ever to buy any books. I can always return a shipment and cancel at any time. Even if I never buy another book from Steeple Hill, the 2 free books and the surprise gift are mine to keep forever.

113 IDN DZ9M
313 IDN DZ9N

Name	(PLEASE PRINT)	
Address	Apt. No.	
City	State/Prov.	Zip/Postal Code

Not valid to current Love Inspired® subscribers.

Want to try two free books from another series?
Call 1-800-873-8635 or visit www.morefreebooks.com.

* Terms and prices are subject to change without notice. Sales tax applicable in New York. Canadian residents will be charged applicable provincial taxes and GST. All orders subject to approval. Offer limited to one per household.

® are registered trademarks owned and used by the trademark owner and or its licensee.

INTLI04R   ©2004 Steeple Hill

Love Inspired®

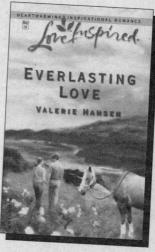

EVERLASTING LOVE

BY

VALERIE HANSEN

Camp director James Harris reluctantly agreed to let animal therapist Megan White test her program with his troubled kids. But when Megan's young sister and one of the teens disappeared, all James's doubts and anger rose to the surface, and he railed at heaven. Would Megan's strong faith be able to help James regain his...and win his heart?

Don't miss

EVERLASTING LOVE
On sale September 2004

Available at your favorite retail outlet.